BILLIONAIRE'S GAME

BILLIONAIRE MATCHMAKER
BOOK THREE

SUMMER COOPER

LOVY BOOKS

Lovy Books Ltd
20-22 Wenlock Road
London N1 7GU

Cover by SC Creative

"Lesli, do you want to take Mr. Boo?"

"What?" I said, turning away from the suitcase I was attempting to pack. It was more like I was stuffing it with random articles of clothing because I wasn't sure what I'd need. It was probably full to the brim with useless stuff, but I had no idea what people wore in South Florida. I would probably need my mom to sit on my suitcase just to get it closed, I thought as I turned toward her.

Mom held up the toy in question—a stuffed bear with a grumpy little face—then looked down at it wistfully. I could tell from her expression that she was remembering when she'd first given him to me on my fifth birthday. Mr. Boo and I had been inseparable until I was about ten years old. And when I had gone off to college at fifteen, my mom had insisted that I take him with me. Of course, I'd hid him for years in the closets of my various dorm rooms. I'd already been considered a freak because I was at least three years younger than most other college freshmen. I hadn't needed Mr. Boo to make me look even more of a child.

For someone who wasn't very sentimental, Mom was more attached to Mr. Boo than I was.

"No, I think I'll leave him. You can take him back home with you," I said, turning back to stare at the pile of underwear I had failed to pack. They were all cotton, some threadbare and fading.

My mom grimaced at the pile. "Those undies have seen better days. You should just toss them."

I shook my head, surprised by her suggestion. "That would be a waste of money." I was probably the cheapest person I knew, aside from my mom, of course.

"What do you think, Mr. Boo?" she asked the teddy bear. "Should we just toss them?" I rolled my eyes and Mom laughed. "You used to love him, once upon a time. And now you're kicking him to the curb."

"That was kindergarten, Mom. *Kindergarten*," I said, chewing on my lip as I tried to figure out what to pack and what to leave.

I was moving out of my small apartment in West Virginia and relocating to Florida to live with my cousin, Lacey, who was more of a big sister than a cousin. My mother had raised us both and I really missed spending time with her. I hadn't seen Lacey in at least a year.

I sort of had a job waiting for me in Florida, but besides that, I didn't know what I planned to do once I actually stepped off the plane, but that was fine with me. I'd spent my life always having a plan and now I was done with planning. I wanted adventure.

A few hours later, I was done packing and, thanks to my mom, my apartment was fully cleaned. I looked around at where I had spent the past four years and sighed.

"I'm going to miss this place," I said turning toward Mom who immediately avoided looking me in the eye.

I frowned. "You ok?"

She nodded and hastily turned away from me. She made her way to my little kitchen and started moving a box. She started to sniffle, and I put a hand out, stopping her from leaving.

"Are you sure you're ok?"

"Yeah, I'm just a little, you know... sad that you're leaving."

I smiled and said, "I'm just going to Florida. It's not as if I'm going to another country or something."

She sighed. "I know. I know. I feel so silly, but I'm going to miss you like crazy."

"I'm going to miss you too."

We weren't exactly huggers, so we just awkwardly stared at each other until one of us broke eye contact.

"Come on, let's get a move on. You have a plane to catch."

And with that, she picked up the last box. I followed her and gave my apartment one last glance before closing the door on that chapter of my life. College was done. Real life, here I come.

I SAT down in my seat and took a deep breath. As I reached for the seatbelt, I realized my hands were shaking. I was terrified of flying. I'd flown only a handful of times throughout my life and I was hoping to keep it that way after this Florida trip. I had Benadryl in my purse that I knew would put me straight to sleep, but I was trying to wait until we took off. I didn't want to take it too early and risk waking up while we were still in the air. Just the thought of being in the air made my heart skip a beat. I was trying my best to stay calm and was practicing breathing exercises discretely when a voice said, "You're not about to throw up, are you?"

"Excuse me?" I said, turning in the direction of the woman who was shoving her carry-on above my head. She was short, curvy and had masses of curly blonde hair. She had large brown eyes and looked a little like a stripper. Her shorts were barely covering her behind and her breasts seemed ready to fall out of her top.

I discreetly tried to look elsewhere, given that I was afraid that at any moment, her boobs were going to spill out and flash me.

I looked at my own clothes. I was wearing worn walking shoes, an old gym shirt and khaki shorts that I'd owned since tenth grade. I hadn't gained weight or developed much of a body since high school. I used to joke with Mom that puberty skipped me because my breasts never grew past an A cup. Frankly, I thought I was more of an A minus cup. To say my boobs were on the smaller side was an understatement, and I only wore a bra when I had to do a presentation or something, otherwise, I was too flat chested for people to notice when I went braless.

I looked like a stereotypical nerd. I wore glasses, had plain brown eyes and pale skin that burned easily in the sun. I never wore my hair down. I normally kept it pinned up in a sloppy bun. I made it my goal right there and then to get a makeover while in Miami. It wasn't that I didn't care about my appearance, I'd just been too busy to make it much of a priority. I wanted new clothes. A new look. A new life. I was twenty-three years old and still didn't really know who I was. I was hoping that Florida would help me find... well, me.

"You look like you're about to throw up," she repeated sitting down.

I looked down at my hands and folded them together. "I'm afraid of flying."

"Afraid? What's there to be afraid of? You're more likely to die driving," she laughed dryly, "Especially in Miami."

"Are you from there?"

"Well, not really. I'm from an area south of Miami. Redsville, it's called."

"Oh... is it near the beach?"

"Umm... not really. Speaking of the beach, you don't seem to get much sun, huh?"

I felt myself blush as she looked me over with a grimace. She patted my hand and leaned forward. "Don't worry, we'll get you naked and tanned in no time."

I blushed again and said, "Umm... no, thanks."

She stared at me in confusion and then laughed loudly, so loudly that people turned around to look in our direction.

"Hey, I'm not trying to get you naked for my own sake. I'm strictly dickly. You know what I mean?"

She laughed again, and I had to smile at her colorful language. She sat back and buckled her seatbelt. "And honestly speaking, if I were a lesbian, you wouldn't be my type—"

My mouth fell open and she rushed to awkwardly reassure me, saying, "What I'm trying to say is that I don't think I would be into model thin girls... no offense."

"No offense taken," I mumbled, feeling somewhat perturbed.

"So, you must have a crazy high metabolism, huh?" she said, staring at me. "How much do you weigh? Like one-fifteen?" I opened my mouth to answer, but she was still talking. "I weigh one-fifty," she said loudly. "Gosh, I weigh like fifty pounds more than you. I think it's all in my boobs and hips. I'm still sexy though," she said matter-of-factly.

I didn't know what to say so I said nothing and pointedly reached for a magazine. I didn't feel like talking to my seatmate any longer. The stewardess was giving us instructions and we were about to take off. I needed a distraction and I didn't want to pop my happy pill in front of Ms. Chatterbox.

"Gosh, I can't wait to be back in Florida. West Virginia is beautiful, but the men suck."

I tried to ignore her, but I was curious. "What were you doing in West Virginia?"

She looked at me and then rolled her eyes and folded her arms across her chest. "I made a stupid decision to go with my boyfriend from college back to his hometown."

"Why was it a stupid decision?"

She shook her head. "I caught him making out with his high school sweetheart one week after I moved out there. That bastard."

"One week? Seriously? Do you think they've been seeing each other this whole time behind your back?" I know I probably sounded stupid, but I was really interested. My life was boring, but this girl's life seemed to be super interesting.

She shook her head and then stopped herself. "You know what? He probably was. That jerk. That never occurred to me." She shook her head again and I could tell she was thinking deeply about her boyfriend's infidelity as she began to chew her lip.

"Let me give you some advice, Slim," she said, clearly referring to me. "Don't spend four years of your life with a jerk from nowhere West Virginia. I gave him some of the best years he'll ever know," she said dramatically.

"Really?" I didn't know what else to say.

"Well, there were lots of sexy guys I could have hooked up with in college, but I dated him instead."

She pulled out her phone and showed me a picture of him. He was tall, blonde and looked like the type of guy who would always ignore a girl like me.

"He's cute," I commented without much enthusiasm. I didn't even know this girl, but somehow, I felt she could do better than the cheesy guy she'd just shown me.

"He's a no-good cheat," she said succinctly. "You have a boyfriend?"

I shook my head.

"Well, you're better off. We're young. We can't waste our youth on stupid men."

I nodded, but I'd only had one serious long-term, romantic relationship, so I wasn't too sure what to add to the conversation. Honestly, that was my problem when it came to most social situations. I didn't have much in common with most people, so I never had anything interesting to talk about. I was a horrible conversationalist unless I was talking about something related to history. Making friends from kindergarten to graduate school had been tough. I just didn't have much experience with girly topics like guys, or clothes, or makeup, so I was rapidly overlooked or ignored by most women I'd known besides my professors. I was surprised the chatterbox sitting next to me stayed inter-ested in talking with me for so long.

And she was still talking. "Who needs them? Know what I mean?"

I nodded. I didn't want to disappoint her by saying I lacked relationship experience. It felt nice for a girl my age to treat me like an equal.

"When we get to Miami, Slim, we're going to get

some hot men. Actually, forget men! We don't need them, right?"

I nodded again.

"What's your name? I'm Violet."

"Lesli," I said extending my hand. She laughed at the gesture which immediately made me feel awkward, but she shook my hand anyway.

"I think we're going to be best of friends. God knows I need some. There's no way I'm going to hang out with my buddies from high school." She made a face and said, "Blah." She shuddered as if the mere thought of hanging out with her former buddies made her stomach turn.

"I saw the ton of luggage you were taking out of your mom's car. I was in the taxi behind you, fighting with the driver... That was your mom, right? The lady trying not to cry?"

I laughed. "Ohhh yeah," I said, remembering Mom had mentioned how the girl behind us kept using foul language.

"You were the cursing girl fighting with the taxi driver. You got pretty creative back there."

She smiled and looked proud of herself. "The taxi driver was trying to rip me off. And yeah, I have a pretty foul mouth. I have five other siblings, cursing each other out was good practice for the real world."

"Five siblings?" I was surprised. "Did you grow up on a farm or something?"

She shrugged. "Or something. My parents have a lot of property, but it's mostly nurseries and alternative energy stuff. And some alternative farming techniques. My parents are wannabe hippies and apparently just couldn't keep their hands off each other and just kept procreating and procreating. It sucked having to share my cereal with five other kids. And worst, they named us all after some sort of tree, or flower, or herb found in nature."

"No way."

"Yes," she said making a face, "So there's Rose, Sage, Cypress, Poppy, and Aster."

"I like all those names."

"Really?"

I nodded. "And it's kind of cool that you all have something that connects you—"

"You mean besides our DNA?" She laughed. "Well, it's nice to meet you, Lesli. Maybe we can hang out when you get to Miami? Are you going to college down there or something?"

"I've actually graduated already. A few weeks ago..." I said, trying to skirt the issue. I didn't want her to know that I was some sort of freak who had already earned a PhD by the ripe age of twenty-three.

"Me too! Class of 2017! Woohooo!" she said, putting her hand up to high-five me. I awkwardly let her.

"What was your major? I was a botany major, believe

it or not. I just majored in it because it was easy. As you know, my parents love plants."

I stalled, "I… umm… was a history major." I didn't mention that history had been my undergraduate degree.

"Cool. American history?"

"World history."

"Yeah, I took some history classes. They were ok." She adjusted her seat belt and said, "So have you found a job yet?"

I nodded. "Well, sort of. I'm going to be working for a nonprofit organization called Ophelia's Angels. They assist the elderly with getting food, clothing, shelter, rides to their appointments, etc. They've recently gone international, so they're hiring individuals to coordinate it all."

"Wow," Violet said. "I would love to do something like that. Are they still hiring?"

I shrugged. "I can ask."

"That would be great. I'm unemployed and my parents are a little bitter about it. But I'm the twenty-three-year-old that has to move back in with my parents, so I should be the bitter one."

"You don't sound bitter."

"It's my naturally sunny disposition. It gets in the way."

I laughed, and it was at that moment that I realized we had been in the air for a while.

Violet smiled widely at me. "Distracted you, didn't I?"

"Yeah, thanks... Wow..."

"No problem. Now I'm going to take a nap. I need to conserve my energy for when I deal with my parents. God be with me," she said, making the sign of the cross. I laughed again and she smiled at me, settled into her seat and closed her eyes.

Feeling not nearly as intimidated by the flight as I did before, I did the same. Strangely I felt already as if my life were beginning to change.

2

"Wake up, Sleeping Beauty. Wakey, wakey," I heard a voice calling to me as I slowly opened my eyes. My shoulders felt tight and my legs were stiff. I slowly sat up on the couch that had served as my makeshift bed and looked around. I was in my cousin Lacey's living room and she was moving about the living room of the loft, attempting to clear off the coffee table that was covered in baby paraphernalia. I spotted a weird looking contraption that had what appeared to be suction cups attached to it. I rubbed my eyes and sleepily looked at it.

"What's that?" I asked.

"My breast pump."

"Ohhhh.... now the suction cups make sense," I said, giving her a smile as she handed me a cup of coffee and set a plate of toast and eggs on the coffee table for me.

"I woke up early with the baby, so I went ahead and made you breakfast."

"That was sweet of you, but you didn't have to go to the trouble."

"Are you kidding me? It's no big deal. It's not every day that I have my little cousin living with me. It's so good to see you," she said, impulsively hugging me again. "I missed you."

"I missed you too," I said, hugging her back and meaning it. I considered Lacey my big sister. Lacey had lost her father at a young age and her mother had abandoned her as a baby, so my mom and I were Lacey's only family. We'd always gotten along and were more like friends, or even sisters, than we were cousins.

"Where's the baby?" I asked, scanning the room.

The loft was located in a large warehouse and it seemed that Lacey and her husband, Jude, occupied the entire floor. It was large, spacious, and strangely inviting. When I'd first seen it from the outside, I'd thought it was going to be cold, industrial and stark on the inside. I couldn't have been more wrong. It was very much a home, from the colorful room dividers to the baby toys scattered across the living room floor. It was homey... if not a little deprived of privacy.

Baby in question was actually a toddler now and walking like a little champ. I watched as he appeared from behind the couch, giggling.

Lacey scooped him up and he struggled to get down. He was chunky and always smiling. I liked him; he was little but had a very big personality. He was a little ball of sunshine, but a very exhausting ball of sunshine I thought as he started chewing on Lacey's hair.

"Where are you going, little one? You have plans that don't involve Mommy?"

Of course, Lacey only received a giggle in reply. So far, baby Sebastian only had two facial expressions: happy or excited.

He gabbed as Lacey held him. I stared at the two of them, struggling to see a family resemblance. But to me, honestly, all babies looked alike.

"So, are you excited about your first day?"

I nodded and reached for my glasses lying under a host of baby stuff on the coffee table. "I sure am. Thanks for this, by the way. I know I don't have a background in nonprofit—"

She held up a hand, stopping my words. "Don't be silly. We should be thanking you. It's not every day that we get a genius on our team, especially one that's willing to work outside of her area of expertise."

I laughed. "Well, there aren't too many jobs for someone who studied world hfristory."

"Apparently, we both have a knack for picking the worst major."

"The difference is that I dedicated eight years of my life to it. You were smart enough to only dedicate four."

She nodded. "True."

"Thanks, Lacey. That's made me feel way better," I said sarcastically, but my tone was joking.

"Well, eat up. Jude's already there. Today's a big day, I guess. Jude's been excited and taking secret phone calls all week."

"Why? What's going on?"

"I don't know, Jude won't tell me. But he has a big announcement and he wants everyone around to hear it."

"Oh, sounds juicy."

Lacey laughed, "I bet it isn't. It's probably just another budget report, but Jude loves drama." She picked up Sebastian who had somehow wiggled out of her arms seconds earlier. "Now if you'll excuse me, I have to give this sticky little boy a bath."

She walked away with the baby hugging her neck. They clearly loved each other, and I couldn't be happier that Lacey had found her happily ever after. Part of me wondered if I ever would too. I pushed the thought out of my head and reached for my bag. I wasn't looking for happily ever after, I was just looking for what was next.

An hour later, I found myself entering the warehouse that housed Ophelia's Angels. It occupied about three-quarters of a mile of warehouse space. As expected, it was pretty dark on the inside and a little bit too warm for my taste. I knew it was going to take some time to get used to South Florida's weather. My hair definitely didn't like the humidity and had instantly puffed up into a giant ball of fizz when I'd walked out the loft with Lacey earlier. I had promptly tied it into a ponytail. Apparently, even the weather was against me changing my hair.

The warehouse was alive with activity. It was full of people busily packing and unloading trucks and boxes. No one paid any attention as we walked in and I attributed this to the fact that everyone was super busy and conscientious.

"Do they always work this hard?" I asked Lacey.

She nodded. "They love it here."

We turned the corner and Lacey led me to a hallway where several office spaces were located. She opened one of them and I realized it was a conference room. "I'll be back. I need to find Jude because I'm not sure who you're training with today. Go ahead and take a seat. I'll be right back."

She disappeared around a corner and I sat down and waited for her. As I did, someone entered the conference room and I looked up with a smile, ready to greet them.

My smile froze as I stared at the man staring back at me. He was a tall, imposing figure. Everything about him was just… well… big. His shoulders were wide and his hands were huge. He was wearing jeans that fit him so well, it didn't leave much to the imagination. And he wore a plain t-shirt that didn't hide his gorgeous, expansive chest.

His muscular arms were long, and I wondered if he were a famous basketball player and before I knew it, that's exactly what I was asking.

"Are you famous?"

"Excuse me?"

I blushed realizing how stupid I sounded. "I mean, are you an athlete?"

He laughed. "Far from it."

I blushed again. "Oh, I'm sorry... I just thought, never mind. So, do you work here?"

"Not quite," he said again. "I'm sorry to be rude, but we're having a private meeting in here in a minute. Would you mind coming back after we're done?"

I felt embarrassed as I didn't have a reason to be there and stood up to leave.

I glanced back at the attractive stranger as I made my way to the door. And I caught him staring at my legs. I blushed for the hundredth time and he said suddenly, stopping me, "What's your name?"

"Lesli Cabot."

"I'm Magnus Deacon. Maybe I'll see you around, Ms. Cabot."

Gratefully, I didn't have to respond because at that moment, the mysterious stranger's cell phone rang.

"This is Deacon," he answered swiftly.

I turned away from him and walked past the conference room windows. I dared to glance back and caught his eyes watching me as he chatted on the phone. His eyes gave nothing away, but from the way he watched me, I almost felt naked.

I didn't know how to react or what to do. I hadn't ever been the subject of anyone's gaze as far as I knew. I'd never been in a "real" boyfriend-girlfriend relationship. I'd never been hit on. I'd only lost my virginity because I'd felt it was a burden to keep it. I'd seduced some guy in college who'd started to look pretty good after a few beers. His performance, to say the least, hadn't been inspiring, but at least I accomplished my goal. I'd figured I'd get lots of practice with someone who actually knew what he was doing later in life, but that hadn't happened. I hadn't attracted the attention of another man since... until now.

"There's my favorite cousin," I heard Jude say before he ambushed me as I walked into the warehouse area. He picked me up in a giant bear hug. He squeezed me tight and then dropped me down.

"Seriously, Jude. You almost gave me a heart attack."

"You're young. You'll recover."

I laughed, and he tossed an arm around my shoulder.

Ever since we'd first met, Jude treated me like the little sister he always wished he'd had. It felt good to be so readily accepted.

He looked a little embarrassed as he said, "So, I'm sorry about the couch situation, but we're going to get you set up at my dad's in no time. We're just waiting for him to get back from vacation. I think he's in Egypt or Turkey. I forgot which. Anyway, I'm really sorry for your current living arrangements. We turned the guest room into a nursery, obviously. Not that Sebastian even uses it anymore. He tries to climb into bed with us every other night."

"That's adorable."

Jude shook his head, "Not at four in the morning when you're exhausted, and some little kid sticks his finger in your nose or hits you in the head with a pacifier."

I smiled. "Still adorable. And no worries. I don't want to impose," I added quickly. "Whether I'm on the couch at your place or hanging out in your dad's guesthouse, I'm flexible."

"What? Impose? Dad would love to have you."

I knew he was right. Oliver, his father, was an eccentric, quirky man and for those reasons, anyone who met him adored him. He was a clever guy with a knack for matchmaking and getting in trouble by butting into affairs that didn't directly concern him. I adored Oliver too, but living with a billionaire wasn't my idea of a good time, no matter how much I liked him. I would be too afraid of using the wrong china or being seen as a slob. Not that Oliver would ever judge me. He wasn't that kind of person, but I definitely judged myself. Harshly.

I decided not to argue with Jude about my living arrangements because he seemed to be super cheerful today. He was practically floating.

"Does your great mood have something to do with today's announcement?"

He smiled. "You bet, but until then I'm going to leave you with Maya. She's our project coordinator and our off and on office manager, depending on her mood. She'll show you how to use our project management system and our state of the art email accounts."

I nodded excitedly as Jude led me to a small office. There were two desks set up. One was practically empty and just had a keyboard and a computer. I guessed that desk was for me. The other desk was covered in photographs of a woman in various exotic places. And around her desk hung various hilarious memes I'd seen all over the internet. Something told me that this was Maya's desk.

"Hmmm…" Jude said as he looked around. "Why is that woman always gone when I need her? It's like she has this uncanny, almost mutant ability to disappear when she actually has to do work."

"Oh, please. I get more done in eight hours than you will in a lifetime," said a voice behind us.

I quickly moved away from the doorframe to make way for the woman whose face graced all the photographs. She was what some people would describe as a big, beautiful, woman. She had generous hips which were showcased in a snug fitting dress. She had jet black wild curly hair and also wore glasses. While my glasses were simple and functional, Maya's glasses were large and red. They were clearly a statement piece and not just eyewear. And as I looked at her, even behind her glasses you could tell that she was the mischievous type.

She sat down, ignoring us and seriously focusing on whatever was on the screen in front of her.

"Yo, Maya. We're standing here. Got a minute?"

She held up one finger. "Give me a sec." A second passed and then she stopped what she was doing with a sigh. She took off her glasses and rubbed her eyes, "Are you the reinforcements?" she asked me jokingly.

I shrugged. "I'll do my best."

"Maya, this is Lesli. And Lesli, this is Maya."

I walked over to her and shook her hand.

"It's great to have you here," she said warmly. "I can use all the help we can get. Should we get started?"

I nodded, and Jude excused himself. "Don't overwork her, Maya. Remember that it's her first day."

"Yeah, yeah. You're not the boss of me."

"Actually, I am. Don't scare my cousin-in-law off."

"I'll do my best."

"Maya…"

"Joking…" she said with an impish smile and then as he disappeared, she mumbled, "Maybe," before looking back at me. "Ignore Jude. He likes to tease me because I'm so fantastic at my job and he can barely stand it. Anyway, I am so glad you're here. We went international and barely know what we're doing. I have so many foundations and charities trying to pair up with us, but I don't know anything about them. So I need your help… mainly research for now. I hope that doesn't bore you?"

I shook my head. "Actually, research is kind of my thing…"

"Then you'll love this project." She stood up and said, "Let me get you a more comfortable chair. I'll explain where you can find the files and then I'll let you get started."

She pulled a rolling chair alongside hers. She gestured for me to sit down. I did, and she busily looked around for a pen and a notepad. When she finally found one she came back and sat next to me and put the pen and paper in my hands.

"Alright, it's time for you to start taking some notes."

She gave me a quick tour of the system and I scribbled notes as fast as I could. I had plenty of experience taking notes, but man did Maya talk fast.

"So that's about it," she said, taking off her glasses again. "Think you can handle it?"

I nodded. "It's exactly up my alley."

"Great," she said, standing up. "I'm going to head to the snack room. You want to come?"

"Why not?" I figured it would be a great way to meet some of the other employees.

"So that fancy, state of the art email system Jude mentioned is just plain ol' Gmail, I guess."

Maya laughed. "I swear sometimes Jude is stuck in the nineties. I swear he still has an AOL email account." She gestured toward a door right off the main warehouse floor. "Right here."

I turned in and saw a little kitchenette and a few plastic tables. A few people sat around playing on their phones while eating lunch. Maya quickly introduced me to them and then led me to a vending machine.

"I know I should be trying to eat healthier, but I love having more body than one man can handle," she said, dead serious as she inserted her change and made a selection of a bag of cookies.

I didn't know what to say, so I just grunted in reply. My lack of words didn't dissuade her. She gestured for me to sit down at a table and promptly opened her snack.

"Want one?"

"Sure," I said, reaching for the bag.

As soon as I took the bag she leaned in and said, "So what's your story?"

I shrugged. "Just your typical college graduate."

"Bull crap. Aren't you a genius or child prodigy or something? That's what Jude told everyone."

I sighed. "No to all of the above. I'm just average intelligence."

"Didn't you finish high school at like age fourteen?"

"So, do you have any idea what the big announcement is?" I asked, changing the subject.

She smiled secretly at me as she tossed a mini cookie in her mouth. "I know exactly what the big announcement is." She pulled out her phone and tapped a few buttons.

"This my dear is the big announcement..." A picture of a game show appeared.

I arched my brows. "Brain Pain"? What's that?"

"It's a game show that has all these fun challenges. Some challenges require braininess and the other challenges require physical prowess."

I stared blankly.

"You've never heard of Brain Pain?"

I shrugged apologetically, "No... I don't watch much

TV. And why are we involved? Like what does Brain Pain have to do with Ophelia's Angels?"

"Well, I'm not too sure but I heard they're doing some sort of charity edition—"

"Oh, that makes sense, so I guess—"

"Ophelia's Angels will be one of the charities!"

"That's so exciting! So, the proceeds from the show are going to go to us or something?"

"No clue."

"So... umm... Is that why that guy is here for that secret meeting?"

"Secret meeting?"

"Yeah, I ran into this guy... tall... good-looking," I said, blushing.

She frowned. "I have no clue who you're talking about. Show me. Now."

We got up and made our way to the meeting room. The blinds were closed so Maya pressed her ear against the door.

"I can't hear anything," she said, disappointed. Another coworker came up and asked what we were doing.

"Trying to figure out who's inside there."

"Maybe it's a producer?"

Another employee popped up. "Who's in there? Is it someone famous?"

Suddenly a crowd had formed, and they were all

excitedly whispering to each other. Everyone had their own theory and it was fun listening to them all, when finally someone said, "I think it's Magnus Deacon. I heard from a friend of a friend who's his cousin's butler, that he's a friend of Jude's dad."

"Magnus Deacon!" gasped one of the girls.

"Yes!"

"Oh my God! What's he doing here? Do you think it has something to do with Brain Pain?"

"Brain Pain?" asked another "So the rumors are true? Magnus Deacon and Brain Pain! Oh my gosh! Could this day get any better?"

"Who's Magnus Deacon?" I asked innocently.

They stared at me like I'd lost my mind. "He's only one of the most ridiculously handsome billionaires in the world that no one is talking about."

"Well, that explains why I've never heard of him," I joked.

Apparently, I wasn't funny because no one laughed.

"Show her. She doesn't understand how sexy this man is."

Maya pulled out her phone and pulled up a celebrity gossip page. We all formed a tight cluster around her and stared.

"That's Magnus Deacon?" I asked, reaching for the phone. I couldn't believe it. "I saw him earlier."

"You saw Magnus Deacon here earlier! This Magnus Deacon!" Maya looked ready to swoon.

I nodded and stared again at his photo. In the photo, he was walking down the street in an exotic locale without a shirt on. I couldn't believe it was the same guy who had kicked me out of the office earlier. His chest was wide and expansive, and his hips were narrow. He was wearing plain white pants in the picture. He looked like a mythological deity because no one in real life had abs like that, right? His hair in the picture was a bit longer than it was when I'd met him. But he had that same look on his face. Not arrogant, just sure of himself. He was a man on a mission. A very hot man on a mission.

"God, he's hot," I said, still looking at the picture.

"I don't know, I've seen better," said a male voice near me.

"Are you kidding me?" I said, turning to argue with the person who I realized was Jude. And standing right next to Jude was Magnus. I immediately shoved Maya's phone back into her hand as if I were a kid caught by adults eating too much candy. I knew I turned a shade of red that would probably be the talk of the office tomorrow.

The worst part was that Magnus just stood there looking mildly amused. Either he was used to women fawning over him or he just didn't get frazzled easily.

"What do you think, Magnus?" asked Jude like the troublemaker he was. He gave me a wide grin and I had to stop myself from punching him in the stomach. He was like an obnoxious kid brother, which was ridiculous since he was at least six years older than me.

Magnus looked down at the photo of himself and then back up at me and gave me a little smile. "Photoshopped for sure, but thanks for the compliment."

I wanted to disappear into a hole. It was then I noticed the other girls looked ready to swoon.

Magnus sauntered off and Jude tossed an arm around my shoulder and said, "Real smooth, Lesli. You're doing great. Keep up the good work."

I shook my fist at him and he laughed before running up to catch up to Magnus. They exchanged words and Jude laughed at something Magnus said.

And then to my surprise, Magnus turned and looked back at me. Our gazes caught, and I couldn't tell what he was thinking as he turned away and began speaking again to Jude as they disappeared through the door.

"Oh my God, he's so hot and he talked to you. I'm so jealous," Maya said as we headed back to the office and the other ladies dispersed.

"I think he likes you."

"Certainly not."

"Of course, he does, crazy woman. Did you not see how he flirted with you?"

"He wasn't flirting with me. He was just pointing out the whole photoshop thing," I said unconvincingly. Maybe he had been flirting with me! I didn't have much experience, so what did I know about flirting etiquette?

Maya giggled. "I love how we were so busy staring at his photo that we didn't even hear him leave the office behind us."

I shook my head. "Epic fail on our part."

I could hear my other coworkers laughing and a few were looking in my direction, and I couldn't help but feel a little unsettled by all the attention I was getting lately. Life was becoming an adventure, but I wasn't entirely sure that I was ready for it.

3

"So, what do you think so far? How do you like it?" Lacey asked me as I set my glasses down to rub my eyes. I rolled my shoulders a few times as I considered my reply. My shoulders had become tense from leaning over the desk. I had a bad habit of sitting with my spine curled over as if I were the Hunchback of Notre Dame. I really needed to work on my posture.

"It's been an interesting few hours, that's for sure," I said, recalling the phone incident that involved a certain billionaire.

"Things are never boring here. Come on, I'll buy you lunch. Normally, we take new people out to lunch together as a big group, but things are so crazy today that we can't really take the entire department."

"It's ok, I get it."

"Well, that sucks for the rest of them, but count me in," Maya said immediately as she removed her earbuds. I had thought she couldn't hear us with the noise canceling earbuds on, but I had been wrong. I seemed to be wrong about a lot in Florida. She then paused and said to Lacey, "Lunch is on you, right?"

"Yes, you moocher."

"I'm not a moocher, I'm an opportunist," she said proudly. "And the opportunity to not have to pay for my own lunch sounds amazing."

"She has a point," I conceded.

Lacey shook her head. "Never agree with Maya, it'll get you in a ton of trouble."

"Trouble? Me?" Maya said.

From the little I'd learned about Maya, she was definitely trouble. She was a free-spirit with an opinion about everything that she shared with anyone who would listen.

Since there were only the three of us, we piled into Lacey's Range Rover. We ended up going to a small, family-owned Thai restaurant that all the locals loved. From what Lacey told me, what it was missing in décor, it made up for in taste. I certainly hoped so since I'd never had Thai food before. Maya assured me everything would be delicious and, most importantly, cheap.

"So, what's Magnus Deacon doing here?" was Maya's first question as soon as we were done with ordering.

"What makes you think I know?" Lacey quipped, staring lustfully at a neighboring table at what appeared to be miso soup. She reached for her napkin and spread it across her lap before lining up her utensils. Clearly, she was stalling.

"Umm... you're the boss's wife. I'm pretty sure he tells you everything," Maya said with a shrug.

Lacey made a noncommittal sound and Maya stared her down. Finally, Lacey stopped evading the question and held up her hands as if she were surrendering.

"Ok, ok. Maybe I know a little something."

"Spill it," Maya said, leaning in. I found myself doing the same. I didn't know when I had become so nosey.

"I'll tell you guys, but you have to act surprised at the meeting, ok? I don't want Jude to think I'm completely untrustworthy when it comes to juicy secrets."

"Hold on, you mean, he doesn't already know that?" I joked.

She laughed and said, "Fine. Here's the story in a nutshell. Brain Pain is having a celebrity edition. They're asking pretty much B-list celebrities to select their favorite charity and partner with an employee from that charity to compete together on the show."

"So? Are you saying that we're Magnus Deacon's favorite charity?"

She shrugged. "I guess so."

"Did he go to school with Jude or something?" I asked.

She shrugged again. "I don't think so. If anything, Oliver knows Magnus. Oliver knows everyone. I'm pretty sure he's just doing a favor for Oliver. And that's why he was here today. Jude wanted to give him a briefing on what we do here and other stuff."

We all had questions and unfortunately tried to ask them at the same time.

"Ladies! Ladies! That's all I know. I swear."

Maya narrowed her eyes. "Are you sure?"

"I pinkie-promise. I know nothing else."

"Fine," she said huffily, then her eyes lit up. "But tell me the truth. Do you or do you not know who his partner will be?"

"I honestly have no clue. I think he's hoping someone will volunteer."

"Someone?" Maya said, giving Lacey a look of disbelief. "Trust me, Lacey, every woman in the world—on this entire spinning globe we call Earth, and maybe even some aliens from another planet—would volunteer to work with Magnus Deacon. He's hot. Hotter than hot. I burn with lust just looking at him."

"TMI," Lacey said, rolling her eyes.

Maya ignored her and fanned herself. "I'm getting hot just thinking about being in his presence."

"So am I," I blurted and then was immediately embarrassed. My words were met with laughter, but I knew I was turning red. I reached for a glass and took a big sip of water. Where had that come from? I'd only spent a few hours with Maya, but clearly her bluntness was rubbing off on me.

"Girl, I don't blame you. I was just talking about it with Lydia, our accountant, we were both saying how if we could find a way to spend some alone time with Magnus Deacon, we would definitely take it."

"Lydia?" Lacey said dryly. "She's very married."

"So? A girl can dream," Maya said, quickly coming to her friend's defense.

"Lydia has five kids and is married to her high school sweetheart," Lacey said for good measure.

"Hence why she needs this dream to become a reality. Her husband and kids are probably driving her crazy. I swear she arrives early at work just so she can have some peace and quiet."

"I only have one, but I know what you mean. I barely remember my own name since I'm so sleep deprived. I can't remember the last time I slept through the night. Sometimes I daydream about sleep. I used to daydream about having a better butt and now I daydream about just sitting on my butt doing nothing." She quietened as she stared off at something we couldn't see.

Maya snapped her fingers. "Earth to Lacey. Come in, Lacey. Wake up!"

Lacey shook her head as if to wake herself up. "I think I'm going to go take a nap in my car."

She took the company credit card out her purse, tossed it on the table and said, "Lunch is on the company today. Don't tell Jude that sometimes I sleep in my car or he'll try to join me and his snoring is way too much for me to bear lately..."

"Your secret is safe with us," Maya said. "Lydia has spent many days hiding from her kids in her minivan."

"Maybe I should get a minivan," Lacey said to herself.

"You don't need a minivan. You only have one kid!" Maya laughed.

"Yeah, but if I had a minivan, I could just fold the seats down and sleep on them."

"Good point," Maya said sagely.

Lacey wished us a sleepy goodbye and headed out.

"So... who do you think will be paired with Magnus?" Maya asked.

I shook my head. "No clue. I just started today, so I'm not even sure who his choices are."

"Good point. I think it'll probably just be Magnus and Jude. I mean that makes the most sense. He's the CEO."

"Or maybe it will be Magnus and Aidan."

Maya laughed. "Are you kidding me? Aidan would

never agree to that. Anything that could possibly mean getting dirty is not Aidan's style."

Aidan was the chief of operations. He was very obsessively neat and professional. He was also no-nonsense. I'd only met him briefly, but from what I knew about him, I couldn't picture him being up for a game show.

Our food arrived shortly after and I wasn't disappointed.

"I think Pad Thai might be my new favorite dish."

"I told you, everything here is delicious."

I looked toward the parking lot and saw Lacey sleeping in her car. "Wow, she really did fall asleep. I guess we'll need to take her order to go."

We finished eating, gathered Lacey's meal and left, talking about who would be the best pick for the game show.

Maya offered to drive, so Lacey moved to the backseat to catch a few more minutes of sleep which was apparently a hot commodity in her household now.

When we arrived, we were greeted by Jude who had a huge smile on his face. I swear, he smiled more than anyone I knew. Apparently, fatherhood and marriage suited him very well.

"Ladies, can you join us in the conference room in about ten minutes?"

"Sure," we answered. We exchanged furtive looks with each other.

And then Jude looked confused. "Didn't Lacey go with you all?"

"Yeah, she's sleeping in her car."

"Maya—"

"Damn. I can't keep a secret either."

Jude shrugged. "I took a nap in the car earlier. Her snoring is keeping me up at night. Don't tell her I told you that."

Maya and I looked at each other and snickered.

"Anyway, ten minutes?"

We nodded and headed in the direction of our shared office.

I wrapped up what I had been doing earlier and headed to the conference room with Maya. I was late apparently. Lacey was even already there, sitting next to Aidan whilst showing him pictures of Sebastian. Aidan smiled politely, but I could tell he wasn't very impressed.

"Well, I'm sure by now that you've all heard the rumors," Jude started without preamble.

"What rumors?" Maya asked innocently.

"Ha ha," Jude said dryly. "You were probably the person responsible for starting them..."

"You have no proof!"

I giggled and Jude shook his head. "I'm pretty sure our rumor mill, also known as Maya, has filled you guys in on what's going on. Most of it was probably made up in her mind, because we all know Maya has an active imagination—"

"Hey!" she protested.

Jude continued, ignoring her, "So first things first, we've been selected for Brain Pain's charity episode."

"Woo woop!" Lydia said making the rest of us laugh. She blushed. "Sorry. My eight-year-old does that whenever she knows we're having hot dogs for dinner. She loves hot dogs."

"Who doesn't love a good hot dog?" Maya said.

Jude held up his hands. "Let's try to stay focused people. Anyway, as part of the charity show, they're going to pair one of you with a celebrity interested in our cause."

"Magnus Deacon," Maya purred.

"Yes," Jude said with a long-suffering sigh. "Thanks, Maya, for messing up my big surprise."

"What? Everyone saw him! It was pretty easy to put everything together."

"She's right, Jude," said Lacey. "And you've been dropping hints and talking about it every day..."

"Whose side are you on?" Jude said.

"Sorry, honey... you're terrible at surprises."

"That's not true. Remember your anniversary gift was a surprise."

"Well—"

"Jude, let's try to stay on task, shall we?" Aidan remarked dryly.

I wanted to laugh, but I bit my cheek to hold it back. Maya wasn't so lucky, and Aidan shot her an annoyed look.

"Sorry," she mumbled.

My phone beeped, and I looked down at it as Jude continued speaking. It was a text message from the girl I'd met on the plane, Violet. I made a mental note to check it later.

Maya raised her hand. "So how are you going to decide who gets paired with Magnus?"

"Well, that's where Aidan's nifty hat comes into use."

"What?" Aidan was clearly never told that he was expected to play a role in all this.

"Everyone will get a piece of paper and a pencil and nominate someone to participate. This way it's fair. The person with the most votes is the one who'll work with Magnus," Lacey explained.

"Can we nominate ourselves?" Maya asked. Aidan shot her a look and she mumbled, "Well, you can't stop me from nominating myself."

Jude handed out the little pieces of paper and I happily took mine and wrote Maya's name on it. I'm sure she'd have a great time with Magnus.

Aidan removed his hat with a deep sigh and walked

around collecting all the papers. "Lacey, you want to do the honors?"

"Sure," she said.

She started counting the number of votes out loud.

"One vote for Maya."

"Woohoo!" Maya shouted, shaking her arms in the air.

"Another vote for Maya..."

"Yes! That's what's up. I'm the best," Maya said, much to Aidan's consternation.

I giggled despite myself. Maya was hilarious.

"One vote for Lesli."

I couldn't help but smile but figured that vote had come from Lacey.

Votes for a few others were announced, but it was clear that Maya was the winner.

"Maya will be representing us. Congratulations, Maya," Jude commended her.

She got up and started giving a speech as if it was an award ceremony. "I would like to thank all the little people—"

"Blah blah blah," Aidan said cutting her off. "Let's get back to work, people."

We all returned to work and I felt a little disappointed that I hadn't been selected, but I'm not sure what I had expected.

I got up to go to the bathroom and stopped at the

vending machine on my way out. I bought some cookies and decided to get some air since it was such a beautiful day. There were picnic tables out front, I was happy to see. I sat down at the table and began snacking on my cookies with probably too much glee. I had a crazy high metabolism and I was always hungry.

"So, who's the lucky winner?" asked a voice. I looked up to see Magnus standing there.

"Lucky winner?" I squeaked, not knowing what else to say. I couldn't help but stare at him. He was hands down the hottest man I'd ever seen.

"Brain Pain? My partner?" he said, seating himself across from me.

I gulped hard, almost choked on my cookie and immediately starting coughing violently.

He got up quickly, wrapped his arms around my middle, pulled me up and attempted to do the Heimlich maneuver on me as my arms flailed in the air.

I continued coughing and was sputtering. "I'm fine," I managed to gasp finally.

He kept trying to save me and I started hitting the flat of his palm on my back. "I'm fine," I screeched.

"Sorry," he said as he let go of me abruptly, allowing me to sink back down on the bench. "I thought you were choking."

"You're not supposed to perform the Heimlich

maneuver on someone who's coughing," I said, outraged in order to get over my own humiliation.

"A thank you would have sufficed."

"Thank you," I snapped, and then narrowed my eyes. "Actually, I don't have to thank you. You probably caused more trouble than help."

"I tried to save your life."

"I wasn't dying."

"You kids nowadays have no sense of gratitude."

"Kids? You're not much older than me."

"Really? From the way you choked on a piece of cookie, I would guess you haven't been around too long."

I shot him a dirty look, but then couldn't help but laugh. He was teasing me.

"Thanks for trying to kill me in order to save me."

"You're welcome."

We sat there staring at each other until it became awkward for both of us.

"I'm not good at this," he said with a disarming smile.

"Good at what?" I asked breathlessly, feeling ridiculous for being breathless in his presence.

"Making conversation with women."

"I assure you, it's no more complex than making conversation with men." I tried to sound distant, as if the conversation didn't matter to me at all. Inside I was beaming and yelling, "A desirable, sexy billionaire is chatting with me! Me! Nerdy me!"

He shook his head. "I wouldn't say that. Women are more complicated. And if I say the wrong thing I'm either seen as a creeper or socially inept."

"Well, are you?"

"Am I what?"

"A creeper?"

"Not that I know of," he said with a little smile. "But I've heard I'm a little socially inept."

"I'm sure that's not true."

"No, it probably is. I mean instead of asking you out on a date, I needlessly performed the Heimlich maneuver on you."

"Ask me out?" I was confused and had to resist the urge to look around. Clearly, he wasn't talking about asking *me* out? I hadn't heard him right. Yeah. I was just imagining things. There's no way Florida's most eligible bachelor had just asked me out. I didn't believe in Aliens, the Loch Ness Monster or Big Foot, so there was no way I believed a hottie billionaire was asking me out on a date. Actually, I had more of a chance of running into Bigfoot than being asked out by a billionaire, I thought to myself.

"You're seeing someone?" he said, misunderstanding my silence. I was in shock, but I guess he thought I was trying to blow him off.

I found my voice. "No… I'm not seeing anyone. At the moment. But umm… you're famous… I'm… not." I instantly felt silly for my reply, but I'd been asked out literally twice in my life and not once was the person a hot billionaire. This was new territory. It was like seeing a unicorn. I just couldn't believe this was happening to me.

He shook his head. "I'm not famous. I'm just rich."

"Same thing."

"Not really."

I looked around. "Are there cameras around here or something? Am I being pranked? Did Jude put you up to this?

"Up to what?"

"This."

He looked confused. "I'm pretty sure I'm asking you out on my own accord."

"Cool story, but I'm not sure that I believe you."

"What?"

I started to collect my things. I looked at the pack of cookies haplessly abandoned and sighed. My stomach growled loudly, and I tried to cough to cover up the sign of my hunger.

"Let me buy you lunch."

"Um no. That's ok."

"I obviously interrupted your peace and quiet, it's the least I can do."

I didn't want to sound like a pig, so I didn't mention that I'd eaten less than a few hours ago. I grabbed my pack of cookies, murmured no thank you and turned to walk out. He kept pace with me. "Did I do something to offend you?"

"What? No. I just... you know, I'm a normal person. You're a rich, famous person."

"That's a weird reason to not go out with someone."

"Not to me." I stopped and turned to face him.

His brown eyes studied mine and part of me desperately did want to say yes, but for what reason? It would just be a date that would go nowhere. We lived in different worlds. He was rich. I was broke. He was famous. I was unknown. I couldn't think of one reason why he'd be interested in me unless it was just for sex. I mean, I wanted adventure in my life, but I wasn't interested in becoming a notch on some random billionaire's bedpost. I knew any other woman probably would have jumped at the chance to date a billionaire, but I wasn't like that. If life had taught me anything, it was that I was an anomaly.

"Listen, I'm flattered, but no. And Maya's the winner. I'm sorry, but I have to get back to work."

His eyes showed regret. "Well, let me give you my number in case you change your mind."

Before he could do so, the door opened, and Jude and Maya appeared. Maya and Jude were talking, but upon seeing Magnus she stopped mid-conversation. Maya lit up at the sight of Magnus and made a beeline for us.

"Have fun," I said furtively before walking away as Maya descended on us.

"Well, Magnus Deacon," I heard her say as I walked away. "You, sir, are one lucky man because I am your partner."

I couldn't help but stifle a giggle as Magnus looked like he wanted to be anywhere but there.

4

———

"Someone brushed her hair today. Nice job," Lacey said with approval upon seeing me the next morning at work. Since I still didn't have a car, I'd caught a ride to work with Jude so Lacey could get some much-needed sleep. We'd dropped Sebastian off with one of Lacey's best friends named Misha. Misha had two little kids of her own and a couple of days a week, she babysat Sebastian while she worked from home.

I shrugged and made up an excuse about trying something different.

"Oh really?" she said. "Does this have anything to do with a certain man by the name of Magnus? I saw him talking to you."

I blushed. "Of course not." I was lying. I hadn't stopped thinking about him since our brief conversation yesterday. In all honesty, I was questioning my decision on not taking him up on his offer. It wouldn't have hurt to just go on one date with him, right? I'd spent most of the night restless, thinking about him, fantasizing about what it would be like to date someone like him. I'd finally fallen asleep imagining him taking me to an exotic locale where nudity was encouraged. I definitely didn't plan to share that detail with Lacey.

"Come on. Tell all."

"He asked me out."

"I knew it! I saw him checking you out. So, when are you guys going out?"

I looked down at my sneakers and shuffled my feet. "I sort of told him I wasn't interested."

Her mouth fell open and she looked at me as if I were some poor lost soul. "Why'd you say that?"

I shrugged again and she yelled. "Stop shrugging. You have a PhD, use your words."

"Ok, ok. I just wasn't interested. I don't think we have anything in common."

"I had nothing in common with Jude, but I married him. We completely skipped dating, mostly because I hated him when we first met. But that's all in the past. The fact is, I love him and we're happily married yet we're polar opposites with nothing in common besides Sebastian. I mean, think about it, Jude is fun-loving, impulsive, and laid-back. I'm a party pooper, a planner, and kind of uptight."

She made a legitimate point. "You're not that bad… usually."

"Awww shucks, thanks, cuz. But seriously, have you lost your mind? That Magnus guy is a winner. Even Oliver thinks so. And it's pretty hard to impress Oliver."

"I'm not interested in Magnus. That doesn't make me insane." I crossed my arms over my chest, feeling defensive.

"If I weren't madly in love with Jude and the mother of his child, I would totally have dated Magnus… not that he would have ever asked me, but you know what I mean."

"Well, I guess I'll tell him you said so?"

"You wouldn't dare…"

"No no… I mean… Yeah, I would."

"You're not my friend." She poked her tongue out like a little kid.

"You're right. I'm family."

We kept bantering when we heard someone yell, "Hello. Can someone get the door? Hello? A little help."

I looked at Lacey and Lacey looked at me. The yelling was coming from the other side of the Ophelia's Angels' entrance. I went to open the door, Lacey following behind me.

It was a very frustrated and angry Maya standing there,

well sort of kind of standing. She was balancing on a pair of crutches and looked miserable. Her hair was disheveled and she was wearing very old, faded sweatpants and a t-shirt. I didn't know Maya too well, but from what I knew of her, she never left the house without looking her best.

"Oh my God, Maya, what happened?" I asked, holding the door open as widely as it could go.

Stoically, Maya made her way into the building, swearing the whole time. She was not in a good mood.

"I hate these stupid crutches...They're the worst!"

I pulled a chair up and tried to usher her into it. "I don't need your help, thank you very much," she barked at me.

I instantly stepped back. I wasn't used to being yelled at and I avoided conflict as much as possible. I didn't want to piss Maya off any more than she already was, so I readily gave her space. I didn't know what had happened, but apparently more than just her physical appearance was affected. Maya was in a truly foul mood.

She looked apologetic as she gingerly lowered herself into the seat I'd offered her seconds ago.

"I'm sorry I barked at you," she said with a sigh as she placed her crutches on the side of her chair and took a deep breath. It was then that I noticed she had a cast on her right foot.

"What happened?" asked Lacey.

Maya sighed again and her shoulders slumped forward. Her eyes showed her annoyance as she started to recount the story.

"My stupid cat happened. Goldilocks, my cat, is easily startled. I mean, more than most cats. I dropped some change from my purse. The change hit the tile and I guess the sound freaked her out and she went sprinting across my apartment just as I was turning around. I tripped over her and my foot got caught on the leg of my sofa. And now I have broken bones. This sucks, sucks, sucks!"

"Ouch."

"Never get a cat, Lesli." Maya's tone was mournful.

"I won't."

"Promise me," Maya said dramatically.

"I promise."

"Good. Now I can rest assured that no one else will suffer the same fate." She tossed a hand across her forehead in a perfect woe-is-me kind of way. I made myself not smile. Yeah, she had a broken foot and some broken toes, but she was being pretty dramatic.

"You know what this means, don't you, Lacey?" again Maya's tone was sorrowful.

Lacey nodded. "You're out of the competition."

"Yes..." Maya moaned as if she was in pain. "My chance to be with Magnus is gone. Gone! Gone!"

She was practically howling now. She started to whimper when Jude appeared.

"What's with all the howling? Did someone run over a cat?"

"More like a cat ran someone over," Lacey said.

Jude noticed Maya's foot. "What the heck happened to your foot? You can't be on Brain Pain with a messed up foot. You can't race on that."

"No kidding, boss. Very astute observation."

"I see you're Miss Chipper this morning."

"I have a broken foot, Jude, excuse me if I'm not a walking ball of sunshine. I. Can't. Even. Walk." She spoke each word with increasing anger, then folded her arms and glared at nothing in particular.

"Well, this is awkward," Jude said nonchalantly. He turned to me. "Lesli, you're up."

"What?"

"You're taking Maya's place."

"What? No... I can't—"

"Why not?"

"Umm... Maya will be fine, right Maya?" She glared ahead and ignored me. Obviously, she wasn't going to be much help. "I'm sure her foot will be fine. We just need to give her some time."

"Oh my God, Lesli. Just take my place. This stupid cast isn't coming off anytime soon. Apparently, my great love affair with Magnus just wasn't meant to be," she said, looking forlorn.

I didn't know what to say, but apparently, Lacey did. "Give it a break, Maya. You met the guy for all of two seconds, that barely counts as a great love affair. That's not even a mediocre love affair."

"Ouch, Lacey. You just don't understand what Magnus and I shared."

"Nothing. Not even phone numbers. He told me that you asked for his—" Jude reported.

"So that we could practice for the game show," Maya hissed.

Jude looked dubious. "And he said you followed him home."

"His security guards are terrible people. They wouldn't let me in."

I grinned. I loved how Maya was playing the victim in all this when she was actually a borderline stalker. Florida was turning out to be more of an adventure than I'd expected.

"Wow... imagine that. Those mean security guards. How dare they. That's pretty terrible."

"That's how I felt!" Maya cried, not catching on to Lacey's sarcasm.

"Trying to keep Magnus safe from crazy ladies, you know that's only their job," Jude added.

"I'm not crazy. I'm determined. There's a huge difference."

"Says the woman who tripped over her cat—"

"Goldilocks is no longer getting the fancy stuff. Dry food for her from now on."

I stopped listening to the exchange as I tried to wrap my head around Jude's abrupt decision.

"Jude? Can I talk to you really quickly?"

He stopped arguing with Maya over why dogs were better than cats, a sudden unexpected twist to the conversation, and ushered me into his office. Lacey stayed with Maya who she was now helping to our shared space.

"Be careful. I don't want you to break your other foot too," I could hear Lacey saying to an argumentative Maya as Jude offered me a seat in his office. I promptly closed the door behind us. I didn't want to be overheard, especially by Magnus. He seemed to have an uncanny ability to just pop up whenever I was around.

"I don't want to be Magnus's partner," I blurted out.

"Why not? He's a nice guy." Jude was clearly taken aback.

"I'm sure he is... but it's just that... you know... I don't think I'm the best pick for the role."

"Well, actually you are the best pick. You're smart and Lacey said you played sports in elementary school."

"Elementary school was years ago!"

"It still counts. Once an athlete always an athlete." Jude had previously been a professional soccer player. The only professional thing I'd ever been was a professional student. And I was embarrassingly out of shape now. As in, I didn't even like parking far from the entrance to grocery stores because I was too lazy to walk.

"I can barely run a mile without passing out."

"I'm going to pretend I didn't hear that. You're partnering with Magnus. We need this exposure. I'm sure you'll do a great job representing us."

"Jude—"

"Come on, Lesli. Who else will do it? Lydia? Ha. Don't think so. And the others are even in worse shape than you are."

"Thanks for that, Jude."

"I'm serious, I love them but they're all allergic to working out. We have a company fitness benefit where I actually pay for their gym membership. Only Maya uses it. She's really into CrossFit. Last year we were all supposed to do a mud run together. You know, one of those grueling races with obstacle challenges every tenth of a mile or so? Well, everyone but Maya skipped most of the obstacles and waited for me at the finish line. And then when I crossed the finish line alone, they handed me a bag of chips to celebrate."

I laughed. "Nice."

"And let's be honest. You're the smartest person I know. You're a doctor for god's sake, and you're barely over twenty." He shook his head and said mostly to himself. "At twenty, I'm pretty sure I had wasted at least three-quarters of my brain cells. What I'm trying to say is we need you. You're our only hope."

"Why can't you do it?"

He shook his head. "It has to be one of the staff. It can't be an executive."

"Jude, I don't know..." I started, ready to tell him flat out no, but then thought better of it.

Why was I fighting Jude? Didn't I move to Florida to try something different? To have an adventure? Well, adventure was knocking at my door and it was time that I answered it.

"Alright, Jude. You've convinced me. You've twisted my arm. I'll do it."

He jumped up and high-fived me. "Thanks, cuz. You're my favorite cousin."

"I'm pretty sure I'm your only cousin."

"Which is why you're my go-to favorite. Now get to work. I'll tell Magnus."

I smiled tightly in reply, gulped and headed out the room. What the heck did I just agree to?

Later that day, I sat in the conference room waiting for Magnus. We were going to start training together, so I was given permission to use as much time as I needed during office hours for our training. I didn't know what we were training for nor did I have any idea what types of challenges waited for us because I'd never seen the show. From what I'd heard of it, it didn't even seem remotely interesting.

I hoped Magnus knew more than I did. I sat there nervously scratching at a hole in my jeans when I heard the conference door open. I looked up shyly and watched Magnus walk in.

He was wearing jeans and a graphic tee as well. In fact, I couldn't resist a smile when I realized our shirts matched. We were both wearing shirts emblazoned with a picture of the Starship Enterprise.

"You're a Next Generation fan?" he said in greeting, coming to sit across from me.

I nodded. "You have good taste. Nice shirt."

"I'm a sucker for science fiction," he said with a shrug.

"I wouldn't have figured you for a science fiction fan."

"Oh really? Why not?"

I tried not to stare at his lips as I studied his face, but I was unsuccessful. I forced myself to look at his eyes, but they were equally enchanting. God, why did he have to be so attractive?

I found myself wondering what it would feel like to have his lips on mine. I wondered if he was a good kisser. He had to be. He was too good looking not to be. I'd never found myself in a position where I outright fantasized about someone I knew in a sexual way. This was a problem. I don't know why the thought of kissing Magnus wouldn't leave my head, but now he had my undivided attention.

I pulled my thoughts back to his question, which I'd almost forgotten.

"You just seem, I don't know, too cool to be into science fiction."

He seemed surprised. "I don't think of myself as cool, but I'm flattered that you do."

"I mean, I don't really think of you at all. Cool or not." I grimaced. That had come out totally wrong. Did I really just insult the guy because I was a nervous wreck in his presence?

He frowned and looked taken aback. I instantly felt terrible. "Sorry, that came out wrong. I wasn't trying to say that I don't think of you. I mean, because I do. I mean, not because you're special to me or anything. I don't know you, so of course, you can't be special to me. I'm just trying to say that we're all special. All human beings... on this planet... so I think of you in a nonspecial way...because you're human."

Oh God. What was I saying? What was wrong with me? And why didn't I just shut up?

"Ok. I'm glad you think all humans are special," he said with uncertainty.

"Yeah," I whispered, feeling like an idiot. I knew this was more than I could handle. Well, Magnus was apparently more than I could handle. First I'd choked and he had to save me, and now I couldn't stop talking nonsense.

I took a deep breath and decided to try again.

"So—" we both said simultaneously. Caught off guard, we smiled at each other.

I broke eye contact and started fidgeting, cracking my knuckles. I looked around the room... just trying to avoid his eyes.

"So, are you a fan of Brain Pain?"

I made myself look at him. "No. I've actually never seen it."

His eyebrows shot up in surprise. "It's like America's favorite summer show."

I shook my head. "I don't watch much TV."

"Yeah? Why's that?" he said, leaning lazily back in his chair. He crossed his arms in front of him and I tried not to notice how muscular his arms were. Even his forearms were ripped. Apparently, he was chiseled in all the right places.

I bet he'd give me heart palpitations if I ever saw him naked. Yum, the idea of a naked Magnus sounded wonderful.

He gave me a knowing smile. "You plan to answer me or are you just going to stare at me?"

I could tell from his eyes that he was teasing me. Magnus was surprisingly easy to read. To me, that's what made him different from most guys I knew in school. Magnus came across as very authentic. There was never any guile. He was like an open book and I liked that about him. He wasn't a mystery and he didn't attempt to hide his emotions and pretend to be indifferent or stoic to be "manlier".

I answered his question about TV, saying "I just don't have time for it."

He nodded. "I get that. So tell me, what do you have time for? What are your interests? Hobbies?"

I didn't want to admit that I was absolutely boring and didn't have any hobbies besides sleeping and eating. Most of the women he dated probably did yoga, modeled on the side and most likely had excellent calligraphy skills. Or maybe I was just being ridiculous.

"Just, you know, watching reruns of old sci-fi shows and reading." I changed the subject. I didn't want to bore him to tears by telling him that eating and sleeping were what I considered a good time. "So tell me about Brain Pain."

"How about I just show you?"

To my surprise, he got up and came around the conference table and sat next to me.

We were seated so closely I could smell his after-shave. It had a woodsy scent that I tried not to inhale too deeply. When I was a teenager, I loved reading silly, dirty romance novels. And so many of the romances I read talked about a man smelling intoxicatingly good and I always considered description to be a writer's creative license to exaggerate, but Magnus's smell *was* intoxicating. I just wanted to lean into him and let him have his way with me.

Woah, girl, I said to myself, startled by my own thoughts. Where had that thought come from? I wasn't exactly the type of girl that threw all caution to the wind. But yet, here I was, less than five minutes alone with Magnus, I thought to myself in amusement, and I was already not even thinking like myself.

I moved a little closer to him, basking in the scent of him and sitting close enough to feel the heat coming from his body. He held his phone in his right hand so I could view it. He laughed easily at the challenges depicted on the screen. I found myself relaxing and letting down my guard.

It was then that I looked up and caught him staring at me. "You have a really pretty smile, you know."

I blushed. "Thanks. You do too." I immediately clamped my mouth shut. What the heck was I thinking complimenting him? Now he would know that I totally checked him out... which I did.

"What do you think of the challenges?" I asked.

He looked like he wanted to say something else, but thought better of it. "The challenges are ridiculous, but they look like fun."

"Really? That looks like fun? Hanging from a bridge, suspended twenty feet up by our ankles over a body of water looks like fun to you?"

He nodded.

"If that's your idea of fun, you need to get out more."

He looked down at me with an amused look. "Yeah, you're right." I returned his smile and he caught me off guard saying, "If you think I need to get out more, maybe you should consider going out with me."

I quickly backtracked. "I meant going out more and experiencing new things. That doesn't have to include me..."

He smiled. "I think it would be more interesting if I did include you. What's the point of new experiences if you don't have anyone to share them with? Have dinner with me tonight. We can try somewhere exotic. This city has lots of restaurants. We can try a little bit of every-thing if you want."

I shook my head, but I was tempted to just say yes and see where it led me. Unfortunately, I wasn't that bold yet. "No... I'm busy. With stuff. With things."

"What things?"

"Important things and stuff."

I was an intelligent woman but couldn't even figure out a good excuse to escape having dinner with a beautiful man. There were so many things wrong with this scenario, I knew a therapist would love to hear about it. Too bad I didn't believe in therapy. Talking about emotions just wasn't my thing.

"Well, I'm going to keep asking until you say yes."

"Sounds obsessive."

"More determined than anything."

"Nope... obsessive."

He shifted a little closer to me. "Maybe I'm obsessed with you... but can you blame me?"

I laughed nervously and pushed my chair back to put a little room between us. His presence didn't creep me out. It turned me on and I did not want him to notice my nipples getting hard under my thin shirt.

"You don't even know me enough to be obsessed with me."

"Let's change that and get better acquainted tonight." I was in the middle of shaking my head when he said, "Strictly professional then. I just want to be able to get to know you better."

I opened my mouth to protest and then said, "Why not?"

He looked surprised for a moment. "Great. Tomorrow then? After all, it's the weekend."

I was going to come up with a different day, but I figured why delay the inevitable? "Tomorrow's fine."

He looked surprised that I'd agreed and stood up as I stood up. He was quite a bit taller than me which was nice. I hadn't dated many men who were taller than me. Who was I kidding? I hadn't dated many men at all.

I awkwardly tried to figure out what to do next and gave up and said, "See you later, Magnus."

He nodded and held the door open for me. I passed by, aware of his eyes on me as I headed back to my office.

5

"So explain to me again how this isn't a date?"

I sighed and shot Lacey an annoyed look. "I already explained to you, we're just trying to get to know each other."

"Uh huh"

"For the show..."

"Ok."

"It's true," I said, more forcefully than I should have.

Lacey glanced at me from the corner of her eyes. "Whatever, kid. If it weren't such a big deal then why are you protesting so much?"

I considered her question but didn't have an answer.

"I'm his partner. If we have any chance of winning, we need to know everything about each other. I noticed that some of those challenges are based on how well you know your partner."

"Well, maybe when you're done discussing that, you can stick your tongue down his mouth. "

My eyes grew wide and I shook my head at my cousin's bold words. "Lacey, you're insufferable."

She nodded. "I know."

The baby was home with Jude and even though I wanted to take an Uber to meet up with Magnus, Lacey insisted on dropping me off at the park where we'd arranged to meet. I'm pretty sure she was just being nosey.

As we pulled up, we spotted Magnus casually leaning against the entrance gate to the park, directly across from the sparsely populated parking lot. I was surprised by how empty most of the parks were in South Florida, at least in the parts where I'd visited. People seemed to so used to the beauty around them that they almost took it for granted, while people like me who hadn't ever experienced a tropical climate thought it was paradise.

And paradise was the perfect backdrop for Magnus. He was wearing a pair of loose fitting shorts and a white shirt. He looked cool and sexy. In fact, he looked like a leading male role in a 1990s commercial, I thought with a smile to myself.

"Wow, Jude's lucky I didn't meet Magnus first or else Jude would have had some serious competition."

I punched her in her arm. "I'm going to tell Jude that next time I see him."

"I dare you."

"You win. I'm a chicken."

"Yep, I know. Get out. Go have fun."

"I'm not too sure how to have fun."

"That's bull crap. You know how to have fun. You were always fun as a kid."

"Really?"

She sighed and sat back. "Don't you think you need to let go of this "Lesli is a just a geek or nerd idea"? It's like you're putting yourself in a box."

I knew she had a point, but I wasn't willing to let her tell me something I already knew and get credit for it. "For the record, I am a nerd... maybe even a geek."

"Maybe, but people's expectations for nerds or geeks shouldn't affect how you view yourself."

"Fine. I'm fun. I'm great... blah blah blah."

Lacey laughed. "Get out of my car. Have fun."

I came across a few joggers as I made my way to him. I scanned the area and there were some kids playing as well. It was a sunny day, but the temperature was in the seventies. A rare cold front for South Florida.

"Hey, you're early," he said in greeting.

"I'm on time."

"That's my idea of early."

He started walking toward a path and extended his elbow to me. In his other hand, he held a bag. I assumed it was croissants or something similar for us to eat while people watching and getting to know each other. With a second of hesitation, I hooked my elbow in the crook of his own. I thought it was old-fashioned, but for some reason, I found it charming. And I had to admit, I liked touching him, more than I imagined I would, no matter how innocent the touch was.

To keep myself from thinking about his body being near mine, I kept my eyes on the path and started talking. "Funny. I would have thought you would be the "if you're not early, you're late" type of person."

"You mean a stick in the mud?"

"Well... kind of..."

"I'm not sure what gave you that impression."

"I don't know. You just seem the type to plan everything."

"I'm not like that at all."

"Really?"

"Really. In fact, my personal assistant does all my planning so that I don't have to."

I chuckled. "Figures."

He laughed and I realized he'd been teasing me. "Actually, I don't have a personal assistant. I'm too controlling to let someone else handle my personal affairs."

"Ha. I knew it," I said with too much enthusiasm. I loved to be right.

"No, you were wrong. I'm a bit controlling, but I'm not inflexible. I don't mind the occasional surprise… And I think I'm pretty open to change."

"As long as you're controlling it, right?"

He gave a guilty shrug. "I won't dignify that question with a response."

I gave a self-assured nod. "Which means I'm right."

"So let me guess," he said, studying me. "You're the type of person who has to be right all the time?"

"What? No." I scoffed. I was lying of course. As a child, I'd had trouble making friends because I had been a bit of a know-it-all. I think I'd improved since then, but probably not by much.

"I believe you. But not really."

"Hey!"

"Let's just both agree to be flawed individuals and call it even. How does that sound?"

"Sounds like something I can agree to…"

"Good. Grab some bread."

I had guessed correctly, I thought smugly, as I reached into the bag. I took out a bread roll and promptly took a bite. It was a bit hard and dry, but whatever, I never turned down free food.

"Don't order me around," I said testily as I chewed on the bread.

"It wasn't an order. It was an offer."

"An offer?"

"Yeah, I thought maybe you would like to feed the ducks with me." It was then that I noticed that he had led me to a large pond where several ducks were starting to congregate, obviously aware that Magnus was providing their next meal.

"Hold on," I said swallowing the bread that was in my mouth. I looked down at the roll in my hand, that I had already partially devoured. "Are these rolls for the ducks?"

He nodded, clearly amused.

"And you just let me devour stale bread without mentioning that this was for some random ducks?"

"I honestly didn't expect you to just start eating it."

"Well, Magnus. When someone offers you food, you don't normally question it, you just eat it. An offer would have been like, 'Hey, Lesli. Care to help me feed the ducks?' Not, 'Grab some bread.'" I was so embarrassed. This was exactly why I didn't want to date him. Who knows how many other embarrassing faux pas I would commit?

"Aren't you testy this morning? Tense even? Is something bothering you?" I could tell from his tone he was teasing me. His eyes held amusement and I planted my hands on my hips and hoped he couldn't guess that he was what unnerved me and my embarrassment over the bread situation made me even more aware of just how awkward I could be.

"I wouldn't say that something is bothering me... More like some*one*." I looked pointedly at him and he laughed.

"Your laugh is contagious, you know. So carefree," I said, begrudgingly complimenting him. I didn't want to give him the idea that I liked him, but I did. Admittedly, I liked him a lot. It felt weird to immediately like someone that I didn't know, but he seemed to be what my mom would call "good people."

"Wow, a compliment. From you? I must be doing something right."

"Just one thing. You did one thing right."

"You can tell you and Lacey are related. You both have a way of making a man feel—"

"Emasculated?" I asked innocently.

"Not the word I was about to use, but I don't want to get myself into trouble, so I'm just going to drop the subject—"

"That's smart of you."

"And offer you the opportunity to feed the ducks with me."

"I'll take that offer."

"Great. I'm ecstatic."

His dry sense of humor made me smile and we spent

the next few minutes feeding an ever-growing flock of ducks, and suddenly turtles also showed up. They were all coming from the water and approaching us with little greedy expressions. In minutes, we were surrounded.

"Umm... Magnus?" I said, moving closer to him as the circle of ducks and turtles encroached upon us, decreasing the size of our inner circle.

"Yeah?" he said, clearly unworried.

"We're kind of attracting a crowd... Maybe we should leave while there's still time."

"While there's still time? They're not going to eat us, Lesli."

"I don't know..." I said looking at a duck that seemed to only have one eye and its wings were covered in dirt. "That duck right there looks like it's part of a biker gang or something."

"You're not a fan of ducks? That's a lot of unfair judgment toward a duck."

"I don't like ducks, true. But that duck is scary. I mean, look at him. Could be running a fight club or something."

He laughed and looked in the direction of the duck. And then suddenly without any warning, the duck lunged forward and snapped at Magnus who instinctively took a step back, knocking me over. As I fell over, the bag of bread flew out of my hand and I fell to the ground.

The next thing I knew I was covered in ducks and turtles, snapping at me from all directions while I tried but failed to pull myself off the ground. And then Magnus's hands were on me as he dragged me away from what now had turned into a duck and turtle feeding mania. Scratch that. It looked like the Hunger Games of nature.

I gratefully looked up at Magnus who was frowning in the direction of the ducks. A family had stopped what they were doing to stare at me and I realized there was a group of teens recording my disgrace.

"Seriously?" I yelled at them and they just snickered and continued filming.

"Come on, let's get you out of here before that video goes viral."

I sputtered as I got up. "This sucks. Great idea, Magnus."

"I accept full blame," he said as he helped me up.

"Well, you should. It is, after all, your fault."

"That's not one hundred percent true, but I'll take the blame for the team. It's good practice for the game show."

I looked down at myself. I was covered in grass stains, dirt and breadcrumbs. With a sigh, I wiped myself off, finally feeling deeply embarrassed. "I must look a mess. I think I'll head home."

"So soon?"

"I think I've had enough of nature for one day."

He looked ready to argue with me but appeared to change his mind. "For what it's worth, I was having a great time before the duck apocalypse."

I couldn't help but smile. "When Ducks Attack should be its own show."

"There were a few turtles attacking you too."

"Thanks for the reminder, Magnus."

"No problem," he said, smiling down at me. He had a beautiful smile and unlike many people I'd known, his smile actually met his eyes. There was no guile there. No hint of underlying intent. He was genuinely entertained by today's activities.

"You're definitely surprising me, Magnus. You're not who I thought you were."

"People are complex. Just because I'm a billionaire doesn't exclude me from that fact."

"I see that now."

"Can I walk you to your car?"

"Such a gentleman," I said with a small smile. "But Lacey dropped me off. I just plan to Uber back."

"Nonsense. I'll take you home. It's no problem."

"I don't mind taking an Uber... it's no big deal."

"And I don't mind taking you. I don't have any plans for the day, so it's no hassle."

I opened my mouth to argue and then thought to myself, why not?

I followed him to the parking lot and I wondered what kind of car he drove. A Lamborghini? Nope. I didn't think he would be that flashy. A Toyota? Nope. He didn't seem to be that humble. Hmmm. Maybe a plain Mercedes? He stopped in front of a car that was completely unrecognizable as any sporty car for the affluent.

It was long, yet sleek and there were weird panels attached to the top. Its body was mainstreamed, and I found it to be very modern and futuristic looking with its wide windshield.

"What kind of car is this?" I said as the door opened on its own, lifting straight up. "Wooowww!"

We hadn't even touched anything and the door was already opening on its own. I was more impressed than I should have been, but the car was like something from the future.

He laughed. "Cool, isn't it?"

"Super cool. And it means you never have to open the door for a date."

"I never have to worry about chivalry when I'm driving this baby."

"I guess not. I bet you don't have to ever worry about getting a date either... I mean you're a billionaire and you have this car."

"Actually, most people think this car is pretty awful."

As I got closer to it, I realized that it was a reproduction of a car I'd seen before, but I couldn't put my finger on it until I slid in.

"Oh my gosh, did you reproduce the DeLorean from Back to the Future?" I said. "I love eighties movies."

He nodded. "I'm a nerd. I totally did." He smiled self-consciously. "It's my pet project. My first invention."

"You're an inventor?" I asked, surprised.

He nodded. "Well, it's more like I came up with the modified design and I had a team create this beauty."

"It really is a beauty."

He pressed a button as he slid into the car. The passenger door lowered, making me feel as if I were in a spaceship. He placed his hands on the wheel and then to my surprise the car said, "Good afternoon, Mr. Deacon. Where to?"

"Jude's loft, Jaz."

"Your car talks and her name is Jaz? Oh my gosh, is this a self-driving car?" I couldn't hold back my excitement.

"It sure is. Well, it's a prototype. I still manually control it, but it's equipped with sensors, the whole nine-yards."

"That's freaking awesome. I've never been in one before."

"Yeah, that's true for the majority of the population."

"Wow, if this is a perk of hanging out with a billionaire, then I'm all for it." I settled in as a seatbelt wrapped around and secured me. "Sweet."

He laughed. "If I'd known that my car would impress you that much, I would have shown it to you when we first met."

"It's not every day that a girl gets the chance to hang out in a fancy version of the DeLorean. You're a lucky man, Magnus."

"Oh trust me, I know it."

He gave me a devilish smile and then the car smoothly started to move.

"It's like we're riding on air."

"Engineered to feel exactly that way. This is probably one of my few toys."

"Some guys buy yachts and foreign cars, but you build a DeLorean."

He shrugged. "We all need our hobbies. But I want to hear more about you. We didn't get around to doing that since we were jumped by a duck and some turtles."

"More like I was jumped by a gang of ducks and turtles."

"True." He smiled down at me again. "So tell me about yourself. What should I know about you, Lesli?"

"What would you like to know?" I said, relaxing as I enjoyed the ride.

"Where are you from? Let's start there."

"West Virginia."

"Oh really? You're the first person I've ever met from there. I heard it's beautiful."

I nodded. "Some places really are."

"Did you go to school in West Virginia?"

"Undergrad and graduate. It was awesome. Especially if you love the outdoors. It's beautiful in the springtime. My mom has a place in the country. I love it there."

"It's just you and your mom?"

I nodded. For some reason, I wanted to share with him what I shared with few others. "I never knew my dad."

"I'm sorry," he said, and I truly thought he meant it. Most people just said it to be polite, but I could tell from his eyes that he was genuinely sorry for me. It wasn't that he felt sorry for me. He actually was empathetic.

"What about your family? Have you always lived here in Florida?"

He nodded. "My dad is a lawyer. He used to be really involved behind the scene in politics in D.C. He met my mother who was from here and moved here."

"D.C. lawyer, huh? That's pretty impressive."

He shrugged it off. "You're pretty impressive yourself. Jude mentioned you have a PhD?"

I wanted to kick Jude. I nodded. "Yep."

"How old are you?"

"Twenty-three."

"Wow."

I shrugged. "I skipped a few grades and was always good at school. It's no big deal."

"I'm not sure why you're downplaying it. That's quite an accomplishment."

"To me, it was just something to do. There wasn't much going on in my town." I had grown up in a small town, but not too far from a major city. However, I didn't tell Magnus that.

"I'm sure there are other things to do in West Virginia than earn a PhD."

Of course, he was right, but I was tired of being the subject of conversation just because I happened to be smarter than average. When people found out, they seemed to lose sight of me and wanted to ask me questions about my IQ, or worse they'd ask questions about my parents, as if trying to figure out whether or not being intelligent ran in the family. Which meant I had to ignore the look of disappointment on their faces when I explained I didn't know my father and that my mother was pretty average, just a hard-working woman in a male-dominated field.

"There's nothing wrong with being smarter than your average person. You shouldn't try to hide it."

"I don't try to hide it," I lied. Sometimes I did, but Magnus didn't need to know that. "I just hate dealing with people's reactions once they find out. It's amazing how people treat you differently when they're intimidated by you. Or they treat you like some sort of freak and want nothing to do with you." With that last statement, I was referring to kids in school.

"Their loss, my gain."

"That's kind of you to say."

His comment had been unexpected and stated matter-of-factly. I truly believed he meant what he'd said. So not only was he gorgeous, but he was also a genuinely nice guy. Resisting Magnus's charms was going to be hard, especially when he was so effortlessly charming.

"I'm just being honest. I like hanging out with you. Simple fact." We paused at a stoplight and he took his hands off the wheel and said, "I'd like to hang out with you more often if you'd let me."

I sighed and looked away from him. I knew that it would be hard to resist his seemingly innocent request since I found myself liking him more and more, and I was running out of reasons to not date him. I didn't really have reasons though… more like excuses if I were honest with myself.

"Ok, enough with that topic of conversation. Let's talk about Brain Pain level questions. You know, the hard-hitting questions."

"I didn't think Brain Pain did any hard-hitting questions."

"I've never seen the show before," I confessed. "Besides those few clips we watched on your phone the other day."

"You haven't missed much," he said, and we smiled at each other before he turned his attention back to the road…not that he needed to, the car was pretty cool and seemed to be driving itself. I felt like I was in a dream.

"Ok, ask me a hard-hitting question that you think Brain Pain would ask."

I narrowed my eyes. "If you had to be any fruit, what would you want to be and why?"

He laughed. It was deep and sexy and it was contagious. Was there nothing that I didn't find attractive about this man?

"An apple."

"What?" I said, not knowing why he was suddenly talking about fruits and then I remembered my question. Jeez being around Magnus was apparently so distracting that I couldn't even remember my own questions. "Boring."

"Hey. No judgments. This car is a judgment-free zone. Ok. Your turn. How about you?"

I pretended to think deeply, but I was really just checking him out. He had long eyelashes and high cheekbones. I wondered about his ancestry. Maybe a hint of Native American somewhere along the lines?

"I don't know. A grape."

"A grape?" he said, sounding disappointed.

"I like to eat them."

"I like to eat a lot of things but I wouldn't naturally compare myself to any of those things. Like I wouldn't want to be tofu."

"You eat tofu?"

"Let me guess... You thought I stuffed myself with lamb chops, steaks and ribs all day?"

I thought about that and said, "Well, not all those things, but perhaps some of those things."

"Well, I'm a vegetarian, so actually I don't eat any of those things."

"You're a vegetarian?"

"Stop sounding so shocked."

"I just associate vegetarians with being really slender and kind of soft looking." My eyes traveled down his body before I could stop myself. I was just happy he was too busy paying attention to traffic to notice. "You don't look... soft."

"Go ahead and find out," he dared me. "I can assure you that I'm anything but soft."

I couldn't help myself. I blushed. I could think of hard things and none of them were PG-rated.

I expected the conversation to take a sexual turn, but he surprised me with a gentlemanly response. "I get enough protein and I work out religiously, so I don't have a high body fat percentage. I know a lot of vegetarians stuff themselves with pasta, but I'm not one of them."

"I don't work out at all," I confessed.

"Well, then we know which of us will be doing all the pain challenges."

"Great. I'm glad you nominated yourself," I said jokingly. He laughed and I was surprised that he found me so amusing. Most people didn't really find me to be a funny person. But I could be funny and even fun. Lacey had been right. I was so busy fitting into the box people decided for me, I'd even forgotten who I was.

And I found it very telling that I was finding myself again by just getting to know Magnus. I felt like I'd been living in a shell for years. I could be fun. I could be funny, but somehow being in school under all that pressure to perform had made me lose sight of me. I had been so busy pretending I was mature enough to be there, that I'd let other aspects of my personality fall to the wayside. I made a decision right then and there to be myself. I just had to remember who she was. Maybe if I hung out with Magnus enough, I'd get to learn about me even more.

"So tell me more," I asked him.

"What's there to tell?"

"Well, I heard you're a billionaire. What's that like?"

"It's boring... like an apple," he joked.

"Oh yeah, it must be so boring being a billionaire.

Having everything you could ever want, never having to worry about bills, being able to come and go as you please must be so very boring."

He nodded. "You guessed it…"

I rolled my eyes. "Come on. What's it like?"

He sat back and said, "I'm like any other person, but you know—"

"Crazy rich?"

"You guessed it. But I'm just a boring vegetarian who works out all the time and loves sci-fi shows. Nothing interesting there. Tell me more about you."

"I've already told you enough."

"All I know about you is that you're smart, beautiful, and you talk in circles when you get nervous."

"You were doing good up until that last description…"

"Was I wrong?"

"Yes."

"Really?" he said with a small smile. "So I don't make you nervous."

"Nope," I lied.

He pulled up in front of Lacey's and Jude's loft where I was still staying and said, "Well, if that's the case, why won't you go out with me?"

"I am out with you."

"You know what I mean. Let me take you to dinner."

I shook my head. "I think we should keep our relationship strictly professional."

"Professional?"

"Yeah. You know... none of this." I gestured in between us.

He looked at me with amusement. "What exactly is this?"

"It's a date like situation."

"This is your idea of date?"

"No, I'm just saying that it is sort of like a date and that's what I'm trying to avoid. And I think you did this on purpose. You orchestrated a non-date date." I knew I sounded ridiculous, but I had to set some boundaries or I would probably find myself in a very compromising position with Magnus Deacon on top or bottom. Oh wow, my mind was in the gutter.

"Trust me, Lesli. If I wanted to take you out on a date, I would. And you wouldn't have any trouble figuring out if it were a date or not."

For some reason, I didn't like the promise his tone held. I was suddenly curious about what a date with Magnus would entail. But I couldn't date him. I didn't belong in his world and something told me that the type of date he would take me on would make me feel out of place and awkward. And as of today, I was done feeling that way. Maybe meeting Magnus was the catalyst I needed to get on track to finding myself, but I didn't know anything about his lifestyle. So far, all our encounters had been on neutral territory. I couldn't promise that I would feel the same self-assuredness I felt now if we were in his territory.

I ignored the subject at hand and gestured for him to open the door for me. He did silently with a touch of a button and stepped out to help me out of the car.

He was studying me. To avoid his searching eyes, I looked back at his perfectly white, leather seats and saw grime plastered across where my butt had been only seconds ago. Talk about embarrassing. "Sorry for dirtying your car... and umm, thank you for saving me from the ducks."

"It was all my pleasure."

From the way he looked at me, I could assume it was a lot more than his pleasure. Instantly, I felt shy. I mumbled a quick goodbye and walked away from the DeLorean, avoiding taking the hand he held out to assist me.

"Thanks. I guess we'll catch up soon." I avoided his eyes yet again and reached into my bag for keys to the loft. I found them and awkwardly stood there, not knowing what to say.

He politely said, "Have a good rest of your day. I hope to see you sooner rather than later."

"Yeah... we'll see each other soon."

He gave me another sexy little smile that made my

heart skip a beat and my skin flush. Dang, just his smile was arousing.

I didn't watch him walk away. Instead, I inserted the key into the door and disappeared behind it as he pulled off. I closed my eyes and sighed. Magnus was smart, funny, sexy, and way out of my league. And the worst part? He was clearly very much into me. What in the world had I gotten myself into?

6

The next day I walked into the office and Maya gave me a mournful look.

"What's wrong?" I immediately asked.

"Everything."

"Come on, Maya. Things can't be that bad."

She sighed and pushed away from her computer, "I just have the worst luck with men. I really do.

"What makes you say that?"

"So, this really sexy tattoo artist offered to decorate my cast for me. And I said to myself, 'This guy must be really into me.' I mean why else would he offer to decorate my cast?"

"Right," I said, unsure where this was going. "So what happened?"

"So I show up at his studio, which also happens to be

his apartment, and I'm all excited... I ring the bell and you know who answers?"

"Who?"

"Some chick wearing nothing but a smile and a man's t-shirt. And trust me, I'm sure there was nothing under her t-shirt."

"Oh..."

"Yeah," she continued. "So I'm like, I'm here to see Jaden. And she's like, Jaden who?"

"So she's at his house wearing nothing and doesn't even know his name?"

Maya nodded her head emphatically. "That's exactly what I was thinking. But wait! It gets better."

I leaned forward hoping to hear something really juicy and I was not disappointed. "And then this other guy pops up next to her and he's wearing nothing but a towel."

"Oh my."

She smiled. "He was so hot. I mean *so* hot. So I was busy eyeing him when Jaden pops up in between almost naked girl and almost naked guy, tosses an arm around each of their shoulders and smiles at me and says, 'Hey, Maya... what took you so long? Want to have some fun?'"

I couldn't imagine being in such a situation, but I wanted to sound worldly and so I said, "Was that the first time someone invited you to a threesome?"

"This is Florida, not L.A."

I nodded my head as if I knew what I was talking about... but I had no clue. "So what'd you do?"

"I walked in, dropped my undies and told them 'Let's get it on, baby!'"

My eyes must have widened to comical proportions because Maya started laughing really, really hard. "You should see your face. I mean, you don't seriously think I would do that, right?"

I laughed good-naturedly and said, "No, of course not. I was just playing along..."

"You are so gullible. I love it."

She turned back around to her desk, suddenly in a better mood and began to get back to work.

"Was all that just made up?" I said after a long moment.

She turned around and frowned. "He did invite me in, but we just sat around talking about The Walking Dead and eating old Halloween candy like a group of losers while he decorated my cast with some markers designed for kids. Apparently, my sex appeal is dampened by this cast. I haven't gotten any action in weeks."

"Oh."

"I know. It's terrible. I might as well be a nun."

She sounded so sad I almost felt bad for her. Almost. Then I remembered that she got more action in a month than I'd had in years of grad school. But of course, there was no dampening Maya's spirits. She quickly forgot she was feeling bad because her eyes sparkled, and her voice dropped low as she whispered, "Are you into threesomes or something? You seemed to really be disappointed at the end of my story."

"What! Me? No. Definitely no." I couldn't stop shaking my head.

She looked like she didn't believe me. "Come on, you can tell me. I can keep a secret."

"It's not a secret."

"Ohhhh," she looked impressed. "So other people know that you're into threesomes?"

"What? I didn't say that—"

"Hi, ladies, I hate to interrupt a very interesting conversation, but I was wondering if I could speak to Lesli for a second."

It was Jude and I just wanted to hide my head in my shirt. I wondered how long he had been standing there and how much he'd heard.

"What's up?" I asked, bounding up from my chair wanting to be anywhere but near Maya where I was sure she would just be even more trouble.

"Phone for you. It's Magnus."

"Oh," I said, surprised. What did he want?

To my surprise, he extended his cell phone to me and said, "Here. Go ahead and talk."

I took the phone and looked back at Maya, who

seemed to be listening intently. I needed to get out of earshot. She was clearly planning to eavesdrop.

"Hi," I said shyly.

"Hey, do you have any plans for tonight?"

I smiled a little to myself. He was smitten. That's the only reason why he would continue asking me out even though I'd said no.

"I already told you—I'm not going on a date with you."

"I'm not asking you on a date. I just thought we could meet up at my office and watch some Brain Pain episodes to know what to expect."

"Can't we watch them from the comfort of our own homes?"

"Great idea. I'll send a car for you this evening."

"No! I meant—"

He sighed heavily. "You're great at saying no, but how about a yes every now and then? I promise that this is not a date and I also promise to be on my best behavior."

"I don't know... I don't think it's a good idea..."

"Why not? Are you afraid of being alone with me? Afraid that you won't be able to control yourself?"

"Stop flattering yourself."

"I don't need to, you do a great job for me."

"Oh really?"

"Yes, really."

And now we were officially flirting.

"I'll meet you at Lacey and Jude's house tonight. How's that?"

"Sounds... fun." I could hear the sarcasm dripping from his tone. I bit back a smile.

"Hey, you wanted to meet up and it's not going to be a date, right? So what's wrong with Jude and Lacey's loft?" I was baiting him and he knew it.

"You win... I'll meet you there at six. See you soon, Lesli."

And with that, he hung up.

"Hey, Jude," I said wandering into his office where he was frowning over a pile of spreadsheets, "Mind if I hang out with Magnus at your loft tonight?" I handed his phone back to him and he stuck it in his pocket.

He didn't even look up as he answered me. He seemed to be completely engrossed in whatever numbers he was looking at. "My house is your house. Not a problem. I'll call Lacey to tell her. She's sleeping in today. All day it seems," he mumbled to himself as he glanced at the clock and then back down at the spreadsheets.

"Thanks a million."

"No problem, kid."

I turned around and ran smack into Maya. "Did I just hear you correctly? You had the opportunity to spend the evening alone with a billionaire and you arrange to meet him at your cousin's house? Tell me it ain't so, Lesli. You're breaking my poor single heart."

"Single? You have like ten boyfriends," Jude interjected, finally looking up.

"Thanks for your input, Jude."

I could tell from her face that she meant the opposite. Jude flashed a smile and gestured for us to get out. I complied but Maya glowered at him before leaving with a huff.

"You have ten boyfriends?"

"I haven't had multiple boyfriends since last year. I've lost my touch," she said with a pout. "But that's beside the point." Suddenly, she got this dreamy look in her eye. "If a billionaire wanted to take me out and dazzle me, I would jump at the chance."

I didn't have a rebuttal and so I just let her continue talking.

"You need to stop overanalyzing everything, Lesli. Have some fun. Isn't that why you moved here? To have an adventure... To do something you've never done before."

"This job and living in Florida was my idea of an adventure, not hanging out with a billionaire."

"And why not?"

"Well, because... It's just not."

"Take a chance. You never know, you might relax and

actually find yourself having fun." She mockingly gave me a surprised look. "Imagine that!"

"Ok, ok... I get it. Well, if he asks again, maybe I'll say yes."

"Oh, he'll ask again. That's a guarantee. Men love the chase."

And with that, she limped back to her desk and sat down. I stared at her back for a second deep in thought and then sat down at my desk. I had no plans to take Magnus up on his offer, but I was intrigued by the possibility.

When five o'clock rolled around, I quickly found Jude and pulled him away from his desk. "I have to meet Magnus at six. Come on, come on."

"Ok, ok, just one more sec—"

"Jude," I whined.

"Fine. I'm coming." He shut off his computer and reached for his wallet and keys. "Someone's suddenly enthusiastic about this partnership."

"What? I've always been enthusiastic."

He had the grace not to call me out on my fib.

"Ok," I said as I climbed into his sports car. "You're right. But Magnus isn't half bad, so it hasn't been too terrible working with him."

"I'm glad things are working out," Jude said, clearly distracted. A text popped up on his phone and when we stopped at a red light, he looked at it and laughed.

"What?" I asked, curious.

"Nothing. Just laughing at my wife. Check out this picture."

He handed me the phone and I immediately started laughing. It was a candid shot of Lacey sitting on the couch with Sebastian in her lap. Sebastian was covered in baby food and so was Lacey. The look on her face said, "You've got to be kidding me."

"He's fond of carrots and he likes to share them. Don't worry, we'll clean up the couch before Magnus comes over." He turned to me and smiled. "I lied. We'll do our best to clean the couch before Magnus comes over, but it might not happen if Sebastian is up to his usual antics."

By usual antics, I'm sure he meant when Sebastian ran around the house screaming at the top of his lungs with empty water jugs in his hand, waving them frantically at anyone he encountered. He had a habit of grabbing them out of the recycling bin the moment someone tossed one in. Jude liked to joke that Sebastian had aspirations to become a maintenance man. I thought it was simply adorable.

We arrived home about ten minutes before Magnus was meant to be there. I jumped out the car as fast I could, unlocked the door, and dashed inside. I barricaded myself in the bathroom like a teenager nervous for her first date. I kept changing my hair and finally just brushed it and left it hanging around my shoulders. I then sniffed at my underarms and groaned. I definitely needed more deodorant. I cursed South Florida for making me sweaty and then decided to just screw it all and jumped into the shower for a quick five-minute scrub down. It wasn't a date, but there was no reason I couldn't look at least halfway decent.

I tossed on a pretty nondescript shirt and jean shorts and pulled my wet hair back into a ponytail. I was annoyed with myself for wasting time brushing it earlier.

I sat down on the couch and waited for Magnus. I tried to pretend I wasn't nervous, but I kept looking at my phone and when six o'clock rolled around, I couldn't help but look toward the door. Lacey and Jude were both in the kitchen with Sebastian. They had been strangely kind of secretive, making phone calls and looking "busy."

I didn't know what was up, but I watched them furtively watching me.

"Ok, ok," I said once Lacey again disappeared to take a call. "What's going on?"

"Nothing... nothing's going on. What makes you think anything is going wrong?"

"Because you keep walking around looking very secretive."

"You're imagining things. Now if you'll excuse me, I have to go to the bathroom."

She then disappeared into the bathroom and came out a second later. "By the way, tell me you aren't planning on wearing that when Magnus arrives."

I looked down at my clothes. I was wearing faded jean shorts and a flannel shirt. Yes, my hair was wet and pulled back into a messy ponytail, but I thought I looked perfectly fine for a night in.

"I'm staying in. There's no reason to go out of my way to look nice."

"True. But could you at least look a little bit more put together."

I rolled my eyes. "For the last time, I'm not interested in Magnus."

"Ok, I won't mention him again," she said, giving up quicker than I expected. Yeah, something was definitely up.

Suddenly there was a knock on the door. She got a big smile on her face and raced over.

"Hey, I thought you had to go to the bathroom."

"Not anymore."

I noticed she didn't even look out the peephole as she opened the door.

"Magnus, come in."

Magnus smiled politely at her and said, "Sorry to

commandeer your TV. I told Lesli we could meet at my office but, for some reason, she was against the idea."

Lacey smiled at him. "Oh, it's no problem. Come in. Come in." Suddenly, she was the perfect little host. I narrowed my eyes trying to figure out what was going on.

She led Magnus over to me. He looked great as always. I just wanted to curl up in his lap and let him hold me. For that very reason, I was happy others would be around. I didn't trust myself alone with him.

And as if on cue, Lacey said, "Well, I'll leave you two alone. I have a baby to attend to." She disappeared, and Magnus came over and stood looking down at me.

"Soooo... how's your day going?"

"Good."

He was too busy looking at me to reply for a long minute. I shifted uncomfortably.

"Sorry. You're distracting in shorts."

I looked down at my legs. They didn't look all that remarkable to me.

"Well, as long as you keep your hands to yourself, we'll be fine."

"I promise to be a complete gentleman. If you want me to be."

With that, he walked away from me and settled down on the couch nearest the TV. He picked up the remote like he owned the place, tossed his arms over the back of the couch and gave me a sexy come-hither look.

I suppressed a giggle, ignored him and stayed seated on the futon across from the couch that doubled as my bed.

"Hey, you can come sit next to me. I promise I don't smell or have rabies."

"Are you sure?" I teased.

"Come on, you know you want to."

I shook my head. "I'll stay here. Thanks."

He sighed and lowered his arms when suddenly a loud knock sounded at the door. Jude rushed to get it, greeting Magnus in passing. A cacophony of voices could be heard from the door as Jude opened it. I immediately recognized them all, excluding the little ones. It was Misha and her husband, Erik, and their two children, a girl and a boy, ages four and nine respectively.

They waved to me and called out hello.

I waved back, but I'm sure my polite smile was colored in confusion. What were they all doing there? Jude and Lesli never mentioned that they planned to have friends over. And before I could ask, more children began to arrive until there were about ten of them and a few additional parents.

As if on cue, Lacey came over to me and said loudly, "I totally forgot the kid's scout meeting was going to be held here today. Darn. So sorry."

"Honey!" Jude said, clearly in on it too. "How could you forget?"

She shrugged and looked helpless. "I'm so sorry." She turned to me and Magnus and said, "I'm so sorry. I guess you guys need a little peace and quiet and that's definitely not going to be here, but stay as long as you like. I'll just have the kids play around you. We'll try to keep them confined to just this area of the loft. Sorry... again."

She looked anything but sorry. She looked downright delighted. I told myself to ignore the obvious setup and watch the show instead, but the high-pitched squeals of the kids quickly prevented that from happening. There were only about ten of them, and I was used to being around kids having worked as a substitute teacher briefly, but between the kids and their parents, all the noise and all the talking, there may as well have been a hundred of them.

"I can't even hear myself think," I mumbled to myself.

"What was that?" Jude yelled in my direction.

"Nothing!" I yelled back over the din.

He gave me a thumbs up and a big smile and I knew then that he was in on it too. I should have expected as much. Like father, like son. His dad, Oliver, was an incorrigible matchmaker and apparently Jude was following in his footsteps.

I looked at Magnus who seemed to be trying his best to look at the show despite the volume of noise around us. He seemed to be perfectly ok with the noise, but then I noticed him tapping the cushion next to the remote in frustration. Yeah, he was definitely not liking our current situation. And I was getting a headache.

I instantly felt bad. Even though I had been set up, it was still my fault. I'd arranged for us to have chaperones as if we were teenagers in the fifties instead of behaving like an adult and meeting him someplace more private.

I got up and sat down on the couch next to him. He looked at me in surprise.

"Changed your mind, I see?"

I grimaced. "Sort of. Let's head to your place. I'm sure you don't have a bunch of elementary schoolers running around there."

"That's true. You sure?"

I nodded and grabbed my purse. "Let's go. I think I'm starting to go deaf and I don't want you to be a victim of the same fate. I can't have that on my conscience."

He smiled and said, "Lead the way."

We headed out and I glared at Jude and Lacey who looked at me innocently.

"Sorry for all the noise. Hope you guys find a quieter place to hang out."

"Of course you do," I mumbled under my breath.

As Magnus walked out the door, I turned around and caught Misha, Erik, Jude, and Lacey high-fiving each other.

They caught me looking at them, looked guilty for a second and then not so much. I shook my head, giving them all a final glare before heading out.

7

"So, ummm... Do you want to try my place?"

I didn't have any alternatives, so I said yes.

It was then that I noticed his car wasn't there.

"Where's your car?"

"I'm getting a few things done to it, so I have my driver today. He'll be here shortly."

Less than ten seconds later, a limo pulled up in front of the house. To my surprise, it had a similar look to the DeLorean, but only in terms of it being clearly more technologically advanced than other limousines.

"Wow, fancy," I whispered.

"Wait until you see the inside."

His driver got out and quickly pushed a button to open the door.

"Please watch your head, miss," he said, guiding me inside after Magnus slid in.

Magnus held his hand out to me and I took it. He helped guide me into the limo and I settled next to him.

"For the record, I had nothing to do with the invasion of children, otherwise known as a kids' party."

"Oh, I know. That was all Lacey and Jude. They looked too smug and collected amidst the chaos."

"You noticed too!"

"Yeah, it was very clear. Even they want you to go out with me."

"They're just married people that want to see everyone else paired up too."

"Or they just want you to live a little and spend some time with a very good-looking, smart, successful bachelor."

"You're probably right. Now, where would I find one?" I found myself joking.

He laughed and we chatted about not much of anything until we approached his home. The guards Maya had mentioned smiled and waved us in as we pulled into the driveway. They didn't seem so mean to me.

My attention turned to Magnus's home. It was a modern masterpiece. Mostly glass and metal. It looked like the type of home a rich superhero would have. I shared my thought with Magnus and he laughed.

"Rich? Yes. Superhero? Definitely not. I can't even swim."

"Really? You live in South Florida. How did that happen?"

"My mom was petrified of water. Her fear sort of rubbed off on me."

"Did she have a reason to be afraid? Did someone she know almost drown?"

He nodded and his voice was somber as he said, "She almost died when she was a kid. She was visiting family at their lake house and one of the adults lost track of her. She wandered too close to the pier and ended up falling in."

"That's terrible. That must have been so traumatizing for her."

"I hear she swims nearly every day now. But I still haven't learned yet."

"You should definitely learn to swim. What if one of the challenges involves swimming?"

"Then we'll just volunteer you instead of me."

I raised an eyebrow and he laughed. "Fine. Maybe I'll learn. If I have a great teacher. Are you offering to be my teacher?"

His words were innocent but his tone was flirtatious.

"Maybe. If you're lucky..." I surprised myself by saying.

"God, I hope I'm lucky."

The limo finally stopped in front of his circular driveway and Magnus helped me out. I enjoyed flirting with Magnus. More than just flirting, I enjoyed being around him. There was something about him that made me feel comfortable. He was great company, funny, personable, and had a knack for making you feel like everything you said actually mattered. So even though he and I were from different worlds, it didn't seem to matter to him. He just saw me as Lesli and that was enough for him. And that's what appealed to me so much. For someone who was a billionaire, he didn't flaunt it. He was humble. And I liked that quality most about him. He didn't treat me like a freak because I was smart. He didn't treat me like a cheap date because I wasn't rich. He treated me like an equal.

"Come on. Give me the grand tour of your house."

Thirty minutes later, he'd shown me the entire house and it was breathtaking. It had only five bedrooms and each bedroom had its own bathroom. Each room had a gorgeous view of the outside given the wall to ceiling windows. The house also had an indoor pool, a library, a fitness center that rivaled any fancy gym I'd ever seen and a kitchen that was restaurant quality. And to my surprise, he had a basketball hoop in the back.

"For when I have a hard day at work and want to pretend to be LeBron James or Michael Jordan," he explained, making me laugh.

"Well, I'm officially speechless. I've visited Oliver's house, and it's stunning, but this is by far the coolest house I've ever been in."

"Thanks. It was my father's. He gave it to me and bought another one not too far from here."

"I can't imagine my mom leaving me anything like this. Moms of regular people leave them things like Tupperware or debt."

He laughed. "Trust me, rich people leave their kids debt too. It's just not talked about."

"I have a funny feeling you won't have that problem."

He shook his head. "Not quite. Want a drink?" he asked, turning away from me and leading me into the kitchen.

"I'm surprised you don't have a butler."

"No butler. I have a housekeeping staff and a grounds staff, but I don't really have a need for a butler. I don't have enough visitors to warrant one."

"No wild parties with rich and famous friends?"

"I'm a loner, believe it or not. And rich and famous people make me nervous and uncomfortable."

"What? Why?" I was surprised by this revelation. I sat down on a bar stool next to his giant concrete kitchen island and placed my chin in my hands. "This is going to be interesting, I'm sure."

He gave me a boyish smile as he reached for something to drink out of his fridge. "What would you like to drink? I don't drink alcohol so I'm afraid your choices are juice, a smoothie, or a flavored water."

I expressed an interest in one of the flavored waters and he handed it to me.

"Let me get this right… You don't drink, eat meat, smoke?"

He shook his head and joined me at the island, sitting on a stool next to me.

"You have to have one vice."

"I try to keep my vices to a minimum," he said before taking a drink.

"Tell me you eat sugar at least."

He grimaced. "I actually hate overtly sweet things. Foods, desserts—"

"Women?" I chided.

He was amused and said, "If I was into sweet women, I wouldn't be pursuing you."

My skin flushed at his words. So he was pursuing me still. Interesting. "I can be sweet when I want to be."

He looked doubtful. "I've yet to see you display that facet of your personality, so I won't argue the point."

"Good idea."

"I aim to please, your highness."

I took another drink enjoying the banter between the two of us. It felt almost cozy. "So you were going to tell me about your poor days."

My comment caught him off guard and he started to

laugh, squirting the beverage from his mouth. He rose to get a rag to clean it up.

"Look what you made me do." He gestured to his shirt which had once been pristine white was now decorated with splashes of cranberry juice.

"Sorry," I said not the least bit sorry.

He found a rag and began wiping at the stains that were now forming. "You're funny when you want to be. That 'poor days' comment was a real winner."

I smiled and watched him dab at the stains.

"There's really no use in trying to remove them with your shirt on."

"Is that your roundabout way of trying to get me to undress for you?"

"What? No!"

"Hmm…" was all he said as he placed the rag down and deftly removed his shirt. I told myself not to stare. I really tried not to stare. It was useless. Just as I expected, Magnus was chiseled.

I pretended to be unimpressed and said, "What exercise program are you doing that gives you abs like that?"

"So you like what you see?" he said sitting back on the barstool and tossing his shirt haphazardly up against the island. He leaned an elbow on the island and studied me while I studied him.

"Your turn."

"My turn to what?"

"Take your shirt off."

I blushed. "I'm pretty sure I didn't come over here to undress."

His voice was deeper as he said, "That's too bad."

And then he did something I hadn't expected. He hooked his foot around the base of my barstool and in one smooth motion, slid me over to where he was.

I was startled. "What are you doing?"

"You were too far away," he said reaching out and tracing a hand down the side of my face. I was so close that if I wanted to, all I had to do was stretch out a hand to touch him too.

"Come here," he said softly. He opened his legs wide and scooted my barstool right in between them. My knees pressed against his inner thighs and I tried to not look down. I tried to pretend I didn't notice the sudden hard silhouette in his pants when what I really wanted to do was reach forward and brush my hand over it.

He touched my face, bringing it closer and then softly kissed my lips. I closed my eyes, surprised by his gentleness. He continued to hold my face as he deepened the kiss this time. This second kiss wasn't chaste like the first. The second one was hot, deep, and the feel of his tongue against mine was more than I could take. I moaned and that was all the encouragement he needed as he lifted me up from my barstool and placed me on his lap. I wrapped my arms around him and kissed him back, wanting the moment to continue forever. Kissing Magnus was all I had imagined it would be but about a billion times better.

Finally, he slowly broke the kiss and I protested a little.

"That was nice," I said, righting myself and pulling away. "But for the remainder of this evening, you should keep your hands to yourself."

"Is that an order or a request?" He was amused as he made his comment, but his amused expression quickly gave way to desire as he caught sight of my hard nipples pressed against my shirt.

I felt a little self-conscious and positioned myself so that my chest wasn't directly facing him.

"Eyes up here," I said softly. It made me feel powerful that I could turn him on. Lesli Cabot was being drooled over by a billionaire, I could hardly believe it.

"Can you blame me?" he said with a carefree shrug.

I knew if I let this flirtation between us continue that I would end up in his bed in ten seconds flat, so I tried to get us back on topic. It wasn't easy. I was still turned on and could feel that I was growing wet. And I gave a discrete look toward his crotch. He apparently was having the same problem that I was.

"So where were we?" I asked.

"Are we going to pretend that nothing happened?"

I nodded. "I think. Yeah. I just don't want to complicate things."

He looked ready to argue and then said, "I wish I could convince you otherwise, but we can leave that for another day."

"Thanks," I said shyly. I'd expected him to push the subject or argue with me, but he hadn't. That sucked, because his understanding tone and gentlemanly behavior was such a turn on. And the last thing I needed right then was to be turned on any more than I already was.

"So back to your question…"

"What question?" I asked blankly, still waiting for my body to return back to normal. I was suddenly insanely aware of Magnus.

"About my poor days as you called them."

"Oh yeah, I'm curious."

He nodded. "I wasn't always insanely rich. I grew up wealthy, but my parents were just upper class. They definitely weren't billionaires. When I was around nineteen, we were struggling to get by, and the other rich kids definitely let me know it."

"I'm sorry. What happened?" I was very curious now.

He shook his head. "That's for another night."

"Oh, are you baiting me now?"

He smiled slightly. "Maybe. If I tell you everything,

then I'll lose the mystery factor and women love the mystery factor."

"Not me. I like to know exactly what I'm getting into."

"That's boring. Life should be about surprises."

"I prefer stability to surprises."

"One doesn't negate the other."

"You're probably right, but it does for me."

He didn't respond, he just took another drink out of the fridge, handed one to me and said, "Care to join me in the living room?"

"I'm surprised you don't have a theatre room. All the entertainers and rich people on TV have them."

"Maybe that's why I'm not on TV," He laughed as he led me to the living room, his hand lingering on the small of my back for a few blissful seconds. The heat from his hand stirred something in me and I was glad when he removed it seconds later. I shook my head and thought for what felt like the hundredth time.

"I don't watch movies or television much, so I never saw the need for a whole room dedicated to something I don't even do."

"Not even sports?"

"Not a fan of sports."

I plopped down on the couch. "So what are you a fan of?"

And then I noticed it. I'm not sure how it escaped my

attention before. "Is that a theater style popcorn machine?"

He nodded.

"You don't watch movies, but you have an old fashion popcorn machine."

"I guess popcorn is my vice and I love theatre popcorn, nothing else comes close to it. So I bought this one at an auction. The entire theatre was being sold and the agent thought I wanted to buy the building. I was like nope, just the popcorn machine."

"You're eccentric… like someone else I know," I said, thinking of Oliver.

"Not really. I'm just a sucker for a good bowl of popcorn." He spent the next fifteen minutes showing me how to work it and before I knew it there was a big bowl of deliciousness in my hands. He excused himself to go find a shirt and I plopped down on the couch while I waited for him.

He came back a few minutes later a little less naked. I missed looking at his chest already. He sat down next to me. His knee pressed against mine as we snacked loudly.

"This is really great popcorn," I commented in between bites. I figured if my mouth and hands had something to do, I would be less inclined to get in trouble by touching him.

He was sitting so close, if I just leaned a little to the left I would find myself in his lap again. I briefly thought about moving to sit in the loveseat across from us but thought better of it. I didn't want it to be too obvious that his presence unnerved me.

He reached for popcorn too and his hand brushed mine. I pretended to not notice how our brief touch radiated heat up my entire arm.

He sat back suddenly, reached for the remote and turned on the Brain Pain. I watched half-heartedly as one commercial after another played.

"You didn't answer my question."

"What question was that?"

"What are you into if not sports or movies?"

"Intelligent women with beautiful legs."

I blushed and shifted a little. I nervously pushed a few hairs out of my face. "You're trying to distract me."

He gave me a long look and reached out to touch my cheek. He stroked it gently and I sighed as I leaned forward, hoping to get closer. "Is it working?"

"Is what working?" I couldn't take my eyes off him. I could barely breathe.

"That's the only answer I need—"

He moved in then. I was sure to kiss me when suddenly the TV volume shot up to a deafening roar.

We sprung apart, me covering my ears and him cursing as he reached for the remote control which had somehow become wedged between us. My knee had pressed against the remote, sending the volume to deafening decibels.

Ooops. But honestly, if not for that issue I probably would have my mouth on him right now.

"So what type of men do you like, Lesli?" he said as he turned the television's volume down.

That question totally caught me off guard. I looked at him strangely. "What type of question is that?"

"I'm just curious. If you won't go out with me, then tell me who you'd normally go out with."

So we were back to that topic. I wanted to roll my eyes, but thought better of it.

"I don't really have a type and it's not that it matters anyway."

"It matters to me." We were now not even pretending to be interested in watching Brain Pain reruns.

"Well, if you're not my type there's really no reason to discuss it. It's not like you can become my type overnight." I hoped my logic wasn't as screwy as it sounded.

"Come on. Humor me."

I didn't know what to make of this conversation and I wasn't sure where it was going. "I guess I want what most other women want. Someone nice with a sense of humor. Reliable. Punctual..."

"Punctual. That's hilarious."

"You're right. That was stupid, but you put me on the spot, so that's what you get for being intrusive."

"Intrusive, me? Never."

I smiled. "How about you? What's your type?"

"Smart, authentic, compassionate. You know, pretty much everything you are."

"Stop being so nice. You're going to make me blush." I quickly tried to change the subject. I needed a safe topic. A topic that was the complete opposite of sexy. And suddenly I had it.

"Tell me more about your parents."

I expected him to stubbornly resist my change of subject but, fortunately, he smiled and went with it. "Well, my mom is a hippie and, as you know, my dad is a lawyer."

"How did that happen? How did they meet?"

"I'm not sure how they met. And Mom wasn't always a hippie. In fact, she was quite the socialite before she found her life calling and did a complete one-eighty."

"Life calling?"

"She lost her sister to leukemia and, after she died, Mom threw herself into adding color to her life... at least that's what she called it."

"What did she do?"

"She dropped the socialite lifestyle, started seeing a life coach. The life coach took her to a foreign country where

Mom decided to renounce all worldly goods. She gave away most of her fortune and moved into a commune in Alabama or Mississippi. I can't remember which one."

"That's, ummm, interesting..." I didn't know what else to say.

He laughed. "I know it's weird. You can say so." He was turned toward me and there was a distinct twinkle in his eyes. He was clearly amused by my reaction.

"I'm not implying her actions are weird. Everyone has to choose how to live their life, right?"

"Right."

"And she chose to live it with more meaning. I respect that. Change doesn't come easy for me, yet she embraced change and let me guess, she's a lot happier now."

He nodded. "She is, but being a socialite was all she knew. Giving up her worldly possessions and everything that came along with it really shook up our family."

I frowned. "I'm sorry. I never thought of that."

He shrugged it off as if having his life turned upside down hadn't been a big deal. His eyes told me otherwise though as he thought back on that time. "My parents divorced because of it."

"I'm sorry to hear that."

He looked away. "Dad wasn't interested in the person

my mom had become. It caused a lot of resentment between them."

"How old were you when they divorced?"

"Seventeen... just about to head off to college."

"It must have been hard having your parents split up."

"My dad was so bitter. He completely shut me out. The divorce was nasty. And Mom was off just worrying about what made her happy. She didn't care that she'd given away my entire college fund to some charlatan of a life coach. I had a resentful, bitter father on one side and a self-centered mother on the other."

"I'm not sure which one sounds worse..."

"Oh, my dad was worse by far. My mom at least tried to get me to go with her. My father, on the other hand, made it perfectly clear that if I left with my mom he would pretty much disown me. So I spent, oh let's see, the past ten years rebuilding my family's fortune."

"Trying to make it up to your father?"

"Yep. You guessed it."

"So, are you happy doing it?"

"Happy?" He shrugged. "I don't think about happiness much. I just work."

"Sounds like a sad existence,"

"Ouch. Let's talk about something else." He surprised me then by reaching out and touching my face.

I sucked in a breath and held his eyes which were filled with heat.

"What do you want to talk about?"

He didn't answer. He just leaned over and kissed me. I returned the kiss, moaning as his lips caressed mine. He was a great kisser and his lips were warm and soft. He took his time, moving his lips gently over my own.

I was hot and bothered, growing wet in mere seconds as his lips moved over mine. And then he was lifting me up, bringing me into his lap again as if he needed me closer. He continued kissing me as he let his hand slide under my top. I gasped and pulled away. He instantly pulled his hand back.

"Do you want me to stop?"

I swallowed thickly and tried to speak, but couldn't. I just shook my head and pulled his lips back to my own, sighing against the feel of his hand as it made its way yet again to just below my ribcage.

And as he abandoned my lips and started kissing my neck, he freed one of my breasts from my bra and began to play with my nipple until it was hard and pressing against his hand, begging for attention.

He shoved my top up then and placed gentle kisses across my collarbone, making a path with his lips to my breast. He teased my nipple between his fingers before pulling it into his mouth.

His mouth was warm and wet and I moaned as he sucked my nipple, alternating tempo and pressure.

I gasped his name and he took that moment to shove my bra down and release my other breast. He fondled one with his hand while sucking on the nipple of the other.

The sensation was exquisite, and I shuffled a little on his lap, trying to press my sex against his leg. I wanted him badly, more than I'd ever wanted any guy. Something about Magnus made me hot all over. And for that reason, I knew my attraction to him was dangerous. Magnus's kisses, his touch, the feel of his fingers caressing my nipples, the feel of his tongue on my breast, was addictive. I knew I would want more, need more.

He ran his hand up between my thighs, coming close to my sex but not touching it. "Are you sure you want to do this?" he asked again, bringing my arms up so I could wrap them around his neck.

He looked down into my eyes and I returned his look. I couldn't speak. I could barely breathe; my longing for him was that strong. I only nodded and pulled him close to me.

His lips met mine again and I opened my mouth just a little as his lips and tongue teased my own. He quickly rid me of my shorts and shoved my panties down before lowering me to the couch. He stood up then and I watched in anticipation as he freed himself of his shirt and then unbuttoned and pushed down his jeans. I reached out and grabbed his impressive cock, rubbing the tip and playing with the drop of moisture I found there. He tossed his head back and groaned. I continued to stroke him boldly and then he finally stilled my hand.

He climbed on top of me, balancing his weight on the narrow couch, tucking me under him before kissing me again. I tried to deepen the kiss, and as I did he used his thighs to open mine wider so he could gently push into me.

My lips stilled and I quickly took in a deep breath as he pushed himself into my wetness inch by glorious inch.

I moaned and arched my hips as he went deeper into me. I thought it would hurt or that he would be met with resistance, but I was so wet, he slid into me easily, pausing to kiss one cheek and then the other as he fully sheathed himself.

And then once he was buried inside of me, he started to move. He raised himself on his elbows and began to move his member in and out of me.

I moaned again and wrapped my legs around his waist. My hips shot up to meet every single one of his thrusts and my femininity greedily pulled at his shaft. My inner muscles tightened around him, keeping him snug and close, and he groaned my name as he tried to pull out, only to be stopped by my quaking sex around his own.

"Magnus...."

"Am I hurting you?"

I shook my head and ran my hands across his shoulders, enjoying the feel of his body crushed against mine as he continued moving in and out of me.

I bit into his shoulder, trying to hold back from the orgasm building inside of me. It started as a dull ache radiating from my sex, moving upward through my entire body. I tossed back my head and screamed as he thrust into me again, pushing and pumping into me over and over. He pulled away from me and pulled my thighs further apart. He took my butt in his large hands and pulled me forward, thrusting into me mercilessly. Gone was the gentleness of earlier and in its place was an almost animalistic lust. And I didn't care, I couldn't get enough of him. I wanted more. I wanted it harder, faster, deeper. And so that's what I asked for, and he complied.

And then he began to come, shouting my name as he pushed into me one last time before spilling his seed inside of me.

He kissed me again gently and wrapped me in his arms. It felt comforting and right. And just like that, I fell asleep in a deep, satisfied, post-coital slumber.

What felt like minutes later my eyes popped open

and I stared in pitch black darkness. I peered into the dark and could see a light from afar and I could hear water running.

I was drowsy, but was immediately fully awake as the dull ache between my legs confirmed what I'd hoped was just a dream. Nope. That had been real life. I wasn't dreaming. I'd had sex with a virtual stranger and now I was lying in his bed? I looked around. How had I even gotten there? Had he carried me? I looked down and realized I was still panty-less and braless. God, how had I ended up like that? What had I been thinking? I was a wanton, sex-starved geek who hadn't used her brain at all. And I was consumed by embarrassment.

I reached for my purse in the darkness and found it on the nightstand. I didn't bother looking for my panties. I fixed my shirt as best as I could, dug around for my shorts, slid them on and made a run for it. I could still hear the shower going so I figured I had at least five minutes before he would notice I was gone.

I reached for my cell phone and pressed the app for a rideshare and slid out of his door. I locked the bottom lock behind me, sprinted across the driveway and to the estate entrance where a sleepy guard opened the gate so that I could exit. I paced while rubbing my arms. There was a breeze in the air that night as I waited for the rideshare that popped up in mere minutes.

I climbed into the car and sighed. I didn't know why

my first thought was to escape, but it had been. I didn't feel like analyzing my behavior. I didn't want to think about what had happened at Magnus's home. I was determined to pretend nothing had happened.

The driver broke me out of my musing by saying, "Um... Miss... your top."

"Huh?" I said.

He had a deep Southern accent and I was having difficulty understanding him.

"Your... umm... top..." He sounded nervous and uncomfortable.

I looked down and gasped. My entire right breast had been hanging out, exposed to the wind and my driver.

I gulped and quickly covered myself. I cleared my throat and said with as much dignity as I could muster. "Sorry."

He laughed. "Hot night?"

I rolled my eyes and grumbled, "No comment."

He laughed again and all I could think of was what was I supposed to do now? I had refused to date Magnus, yet I had jumped into bed with him at the first opportunity. What must he think of me? I closed my eyes and took a deep breath. I didn't know what tomorrow held, but I knew I was a huge chicken and would avoid finding out.

8

I was taking a sick day. By sick day, I meant I was hiding out at Oliver's house while he was still on vacation and I was avoiding all calls from a certain sexy billionaire.

I felt like a coward, but that was understandable because I was a coward. I didn't want to go to work because I was sure I'd run into Magnus there.

He had called me over and over while I was in the car with the driver. I'd ignored the calls, but then I started getting text messages. Most of them wanted to know what was wrong, where I was and what was going on. I answered none of them and promptly deleted all the voicemails.

When I'd arrived home, I received another text that said, "Please respond. I just want to make sure you're ok."

The text made me feel instantly guilty, so I responded with: "I'm fine. Just got home."

He texted me again. "Why did you leave?"

I pointedly ignored that text.

I'd felt grumpy and confused this morning, so I'd been ecstatic when Violet texted me asking me if I had plans today. I had said no, and so she and I agreed to meet at Oliver's house.

She came trekking up Oliver's property fanning herself and breathing heavily. For some reason that no one knew or understood, Oliver did not allow other people's cars on his property. He was a quirky old man, so we didn't understand his reasoning for most of the things he did.

Violet was wearing a white mini dress and sneakers. She looked adorable. If I walked around in a mini dress and sneakers, I would look like a fashion disaster. She stopped fanning herself and gave me a huge smile when she spotted me.

"What's up, buddy?" she said making me smile.

"Hey there... sorry for the hike." I stood up to meet her.

"Whatever, it's like being Cinderella or whichever the rich one was. This place is freaking amazing. I can't believe I'm hanging out at a billionaire's house. This is freaking awesome."

Her excitement was contagious as she asked me to

show her around. We went from room to room with her gasping, oohing and ahhing, and taking selfies in various rooms of the house. I just hoped she didn't put them on Facebook. I didn't think Oliver would be ok with that.

We finally ended up back in one of the living rooms toward the back of Oliver's house that overlooked the pool.

"Man, I never figured you for the type to skip out on work. Do you hate it?" she asked, catching me off guard again with her bluntness.

"No. I don't hate it. I just needed a break."

She sat down next to me and tossed her feet up on the coffee table that was probably more expensive than all my student loans combined.

"Is it one of those nonprofits where everyone thinks they work harder than the other person? And so everyone has some sort of savior complex?"

"No. Definitely not. They're great. I love working there."

She sighed. "I haven't found a job yet. And I desperately need one. Mom and Dad are driving me crazy." She looked at me with a hopeful expression. "Do you think maybe you could put in a good word for me at your job... maybe they might be interested in hiring me?"

"Of course. I meant to do that ages ago, but I got... distracted." I didn't tell her that the distraction had been in the form of a certain very good-looking billionaire.

She smiled brightly, "Thanks, Les. I'd really appreciate it."

We spent the rest of the day lounging around Oliver's pool. It was nice having a friend to talk to about nothing of importance. I hadn't made any lasting friendships while in school and I realized that at that moment in my life, Violet was my only friend.

We were both silently sitting around daydreaming, just enjoying the weather, when she announced, "I heard on TV that Magnus Deacon is in town."

I wrinkled my nose. It was like I just couldn't win. "Really?"

"Yeah. I heard he's in town for some charity event. You do know who Magnus Deacon is, right?"

"Of course, I do." I grudgingly added, "We've met."

"No way… what?" she sputtered, sitting up dramatically. She ripped her sunglasses off. "You met Magnus Deacon and you didn't tell me? How? Where? Oh my gosh, is he as sexy in person as he is on television?"

I shrugged and tried to appear nonchalant as I underplayed just how sexy Magnus was. "I guess he's alright looking."

She looked at me incredulously. "Alright looking? The man looks like a Greek god. He's tall, sexy, beautiful eyes... beautiful teeth."

"Beautiful teeth?" I couldn't help but laugh. "Yeah, he does have a great smile," I said, not noticing until that moment that the thought of his smile made me smile as well.

"Tell me *everything*. How did you meet him? Is he charming? No, no, most importantly, is he single?"

"Uhh..." I didn't know how to answer that without sounding like a crazy jealous stalker. What was I supposed to say? He's single, but hands off? I thought I didn't care about who Magnus dated, but jealousy reared its ugly head when I thought about him dating someone other than me. Especially when that someone was a person I considered a friend. I inwardly groaned at how conflicted my feelings for Magnus were: I didn't want to date him, but I didn't want anyone else to have him either. Great. That was so illogical.

"Come on, come on, tell me everything. I'm practically salivating over here. It's not every day that you realize you know someone who knows not one but two billionaires and one of them is a really hot, eligible, tasty, billionaire."

"Tasty?" I laughed at the description. I couldn't help myself from thinking: Sex with Magnus had been pretty incredible, but tasty definitely was not an adjective I'd use to describe him.

Violet smacked her lips together. "Yes, tasty. Do you know all the things I would do to that man? Girl, one night with me and he would have to limp to work." I nearly fell out of my chair laughing. And she began to laugh too.

"Oh my gosh, you are so ridiculous. I mean that in a nice way. I hope you get hired. I have a coworker named Maya and I think you two would really hit it off."

"I'm sure Maya's great, but tell me more about Magnus Deacon. How did you meet him? Is he a friend of Mr. Oliver's?"

I nodded. "I think so. I'm not too sure of their relationship, but I know that they know each other. I actually met Magnus at work."

"What?" her eyes became huge again.

"You know that charity event you heard about in the news? Well, Ophelia's Angels is that charity."

"No. You're joking?" She could barely contain herself. "Are you working with him?"

"Yes."

"Wow. Just wow. That is so cool. Can you introduce us?" she said, suddenly grabbing my arm. "It would make Steve so jealous if he saw me in the tabloids with Magnus Deacon."

"I guess I could. He doesn't really work with us, he just comes in and out. I'm sort of his partner for the show Brain Pain." I explained to her about the charity event and how Magnus was involved.

"I need to hang out with you more often. You're like the luckiest girl I know."

"I wouldn't say that exactly."

"I would. Now tell me everything. What's he like?"

I shrugged. "Nice, I guess."

She looked at me as if I had no clue what I was talking about. "Nice, that's all? Nice is the word I use to describe the mailman. Come on, what's he really like?" She emphasized the word 'really'.

I thought about her question and then said, "He's easy-going, patient, a genuinely good guy. He's not like anyone I've ever met before. He's rich, but not arrogant. He's good-looking, but doesn't seem to care. He's smart with a wry sense of humor. He's observant, considerate. And persistent." I smiled a little, thinking of the number of times he'd asked me out despite rejection after rejection.

She sighed and sat back in her chair. "He sounds perfect. Do you think he's dating anyone?"

I instantly tensed up. Was she really interested in pursuing him? I felt uneasy about the idea, but I'd made it clear that I didn't want anything to do with him on a personal level. Funny, I'd decided that after spending the evening getting to know him on a very, very personal level. But I was determined to pretend that night didn't happen.

"I don't think he's dating anyone." I definitely didn't mention that he'd asked me out countless times. I didn't feel like explaining to her or anyone else why I'd said no, but then again, I couldn't even explain to myself why I'd said no. I didn't know what my problem was, but I didn't want anyone else to think I was a complete basket case, either.

"Cool. So do you think you could introduce us?"

Now I wasn't going to do that. I didn't want to be with him, but I surely didn't want a friend of mine to sneak in on my territory. I bit the inside of my cheek; I knew I was being unfair and I had no claim on Magnus and, of course, I wasn't going to tell Violet that I'd slept with him, but I certainly wasn't going to help her date him.

"I don't know him all that well," I lied. "I'm just his partner. But I'm sure you'll meet him eventually if you're hired. He pops up from time to time." In my head, I was hoping the opposite. I was hoping he and Violet would never meet. He would take one look at her and forget I even existed. I was Plain Jane while Violet looked like a modern-day Marilyn Monroe. I didn't know what I was feeling. I didn't want him, but I didn't want anyone else to have him either.

Who was I kidding? I did want him. Well, in a sexual sense. I didn't want a relationship with him. Being in a relationship with a billionaire would be way too complicated, right? And complication wasn't what I needed in my life. I wanted adventure, but not complications. I didn't need Magnus.

But if that were true why did the idea of him and Violet together fill me with jealousy?

"Well, I hope to get to meet him."

Before I could control myself, I blurted out, "He asked me out." Wow, it's amazing what a little jealousy will make you do, I thought to myself immediately regretting telling Violet. But hey, she didn't know the full story... yet. I just needed to keep my mouth shut.

"Seriously? And you never said a word about it until just now. Are you freaking kidding me? When did this all happen? You should have told me about it ages ago."

"It was no big deal. I turned him down."

Her mouth literally fell open. "Are you insane?"

"What?"

"Are you insane?"

"I heard you the first time. Why are you questioning my sanity? What did I do?"

Violet narrowed her eyes at me. "What do you mean what did you do? You turned down Magnus Deacon. *Magnus Deacon*," she repeated for emphasis.

I sighed, deeply regretting my sudden outburst. "I think I need a makeover," I said in an obvious attempt to change the subject.

Violet called me out immediately. "Hey, hey, hey, don't change the subject."

"I'm not... I mean... just look at me and now look at you."

She looked at her clothes and shrugged. "What? I mean, yeah, you could put on a little makeup and maybe wear clothes that actually fit... but you look fine." Then she paused and gave me a disappointed look. "Don't tell me you said no to Magnus Deacon, this state's most eligible bachelor, because you're insecure about your looks."

"What? No! I'm not insecure. I'm just, well... look at me."

"There's nothing wrong with you."

I sighed. "I haven't used lotion in about six months."

"Yikes. Now that is a little much."

"But seriously, Magnus Deacon isn't my type."

She looked at me dubiously. "You have a type?"

"Of course, I do."

She crossed her arms. "Alright let's hear it."

I tried to come up with something but my mind went blank. "Umm... let's just say, I do have a type and Magnus really doesn't fall under that umbrella."

"Got it. Rich. Sexy. Powerful. Not your type."

"Right."

"So I guess poor, unattractive, and powerless is more your speed?"

"Hey!"

I was offended, but I didn't want to tell her that I felt Magnus was too far out of my league, not to mention out of my comfort zone, romantically. I was just an average girl from West Virginia. Magnus could pretty much chew me up and spit me out. Yeah, he was a nice guy, but that didn't change the fact I was inexperienced and intimidated by his wealth. Not to mention, my experience with relationships was limited. I had just enough experience to lose my virginity, but that was about all. Before I'd slept with Magnus, I'd only slept with one other guy.

I'd had a boyfriend in graduate school, but I preferred to use that term loosely. He'd been a guy, but he hadn't been much of a friend or lover. He'd been a bit of a dork. I hated how he chewed with his mouth full and his skills in the bedroom had been desperately lacking. I remember spending evenings online reading about sex to find a way to tell him how terrible he was and, in the end, we'd just broken up. He told me I was cold and inexperienced so it was my fault I hadn't been satisfied. I knew he was wrong, but his words had still hurt.

"Can we talk about something else?" I didn't want to dwell on my own insecurities.

"Like what?"

"How are your siblings doing? They must be glad to have you home."

She looked sad for a moment. "They're great, but being home is making me feel like a loser. And even worse my younger sister has been offered a job at NASA in Alabama."

I laughed. "How is that bad news?"

"I'm the oldest! I should be the overachiever. Instead, my little sister is... Gosh, she sucks."

I nudged Violet. "Be nice. You should be happy for her."

She made a face and changed the subject. "So are you serious about that makeover?"

I nodded. "I would at least like to get some new clothes. Maybe something with some color and no holes."

Violet nodded. "Good idea. Let's do this."

"You mean now?"

"You got other plans for today?"

"Nope."

"Then let's go."

We took Violet's car to the mall. I was taken by surprise when we arrived at the mall to find it full of people. It was completely unexpected especially since it was a weekday. I remember reading an article about how malls were closing down and disappearing around America. Apparently, those journalists or reporters didn't get the memo: malls were still booming and even thriving in some areas.

"I haven't hung out at a mall since, I don't know, I was maybe fifteen."

We made our way to the entrance of a large department store, one of the last of a dying breed.

"Same here," Violet said. "Kids from my school would hang out here all the time, but I was rarely invited."

Her comment made me pause. "Were you bullied in high school?"

She shook her head. "I wasn't bullied. Just ignored. Believe it or not, I sort of have trouble making friends. I don't know why. I think I'm pretty great."

Violet could be a little much and sometimes she said things that were totally off-the-wall cuckoo, but I thought she was cool and funny.

"I think other girls were just intimidated by my beauty," she said matter-of-factly. She noticed the look on my face and immediately laughed.

"I was joking!" She sighed. "I pretty much struggled with my weight all my life. I wasn't exactly what you would call hot in high school. I was still pretty outgoing, but being chubby definitely made me feel insecure at times. I think some of the kids picked up on that and were determined to make my life miserable by pretending that I just didn't exist."

I looked at her in surprise. "I'm sorry that happened to you. You look great now and I'm sure you were beautiful then, no matter your size."

She smiled. "Thanks. That's probably the nicest thing another woman has ever said to me. I appreciate that, but to maintain this figure I have to work out at least five days a week and watch what I eat. Carbs hate me, but I love them so much. It's tough. The struggle is all too real."

"That sucks."

"Sure does. I was such a chubby teen. I loved cinnamon rolls... all the sugar and cinnamon on such a tasty treat. Yum," she said, making me laugh. "But when college rolled around, I started taking nutrition classes and I discovered that I actually do like working out. Who would have known? And so the more weight I lost, the fewer clothes I wore," she said with a giggle. "Body confidence is amaaazing," she drawled, stretching out the word. "Like seriously, Les. Nothing feels better than being confident in your own skin. And I kind of wish you would realize that."

"What?"

"Well, I noticed how you always try to cover your body up and try to blend in. It's sort of like you're afraid of being noticed."

I opened my mouth to argue with her and then closed it. She was right. Who would have known Violet was so perceptive?

I decided to just deny the truth that Violet could easily see. "I'm not afraid of being noticed. I'm just modest, that's all. There's nothing wrong with that." I knew my comment came out sounding a tad defensive. I did feel a little attacked, but only because her assessment was spot on.

"Hey, don't bite my head off. I'm not saying you have to dress like me, but there's nothing wrong with accepting your sexual side and even flaunting it a little."

I blushed. If only she knew I had spent quite a bit of my evening accepting my sexual side and flaunting it all over Magnus. But maybe she was right.

"What exactly are you suggesting? Make out with random dudes and wear mini-skirts?"

"What? No. That's totally my role in this friendship. I'm the slutty friend," she joked.

Her comment made me laugh. "So what am I?"

"The smart and pretty friend who desperately needs a makeover or at least a good haircut and clothes from this decade."

She had a point there. I was wearing a pair of shorts I used to wear in high school and the t-shirt was from some event I went to in college. And the sad part was that I'd changed into the clothes I currently had on to look "nice." It was clear: I had no fashion sense.

"I always cut my hair at home," was all I could think to say. "I think it comes out pretty good."

She gasped and mockingly widened her eyes. "This has got to stop."

I laughed again. Violet was hilarious. "Well, you win. New haircut and new clothes sound like a good idea."

"Hallelujah. Follow me."

9

The next day, I rode with Lacey to the office. I was still a little uncomfortable and nervous about my new look. My hair was still long, but it had gotten a much-needed trim and I had actually brushed it. When I'd mentioned I wanted to put some color in my wardrobe, Violet had been ecstatic. Now I was the proud owner of clothes that weren't just khaki or faded.

My once colorless wardrobe now had sprinkles of blue, pink, red, and even a little bit of yellow. I thought yellow washed me out, but Violet said all colors were meant to be worn. I didn't quite trust that fashion advice, but what did I know? I'd lived in jean shorts, jeans and flannel shirts for eight years straight. My wardrobe was practically crying for an update.

I pulled at the red polka dot skirt Violet had convinced me to wear. It was really snug and I was surprised that it actually looked pretty great on my rear end. I hadn't considered my rear end an asset until Violet had said, "You have some junk in your trunk, girl," and high-fived me.

I was wearing a graphic tee with the skirt which Violet said was totally fine. I loved the whole graphic tee look and liked that I could wear it with a professional skirt and still look put together. I felt like myself, just a dressier version.

I nervously pulled at my hair. And then I nervously pulled at the tight skirt I was wearing and finally, I fidgeted with the clingy, long-sleeve, graphic shirt I had on.

"Stop fidgeting. You look great," Lacey said, not for the first time. She'd helped me pick out this morning's outfit.

"You really think so? I don't know," I said as I looked down at my new shoes, pointy-toed, red, and adorable. "I don't know. I just don't feel completely like myself."

"Trust me. You look like you, just an updated version. Like Lesli 2.0 instead of Lesli 1.0."

"Thanks... I guess."

She laughed at my dubious tone as she impatiently waited for the stoplight to change. She lowered the sun visor and looked at the little mirror inside. "Ugghhh," she groaned at her reflection, as she flipped the sun visor back up and said with a voice full of disgust. "I gotta get more sleep. I think I'm starting to get bags under my eyes."

I shook my head. "You're crazy. We have great genes. We don't get bags. It's all in your mind."

She whimpered as she pulled away from the stoplight. "Don't humor me. I'm falling apart, but whatever." Then she perked up. "Anyway, we're not talking about me."

I groaned inwardly. I had hoped that the topic of conversation would continue to be the nonexistent bags under her eyes instead of my makeover.

"Seriously, you look good. You're wearing clothes that actually fit and something other than a t-shirt. And your hair is freshly cut. You're actually making me envious. I haven't cut my hair in at least a year and I'm pretty sure it's covered in baby drool half the time. Sebastian loves to eat my hair."

"You look great. You're a hot mom."

She beamed. "You think so?"

"Definitely."

"You aren't just saying that to make me feel good about not showering or washing my hair in days?"

I laughed. "I didn't need to know all that information, but, umm, no... I'm not just complimenting you to appease you... It's a genuine compliment. You're a great mom and you make motherhood look good."

She placed her hand over her heart and said, "That's

soooo sweet. I knew there was a reason you were my favorite cousin."

"I'm your only cousin."

She giggled and I punched her lightly in the shoulder.

"What do you think the chances are that Jude will hire Violet?"

"One hundred percent."

"Oh. Those are good chances."

"Yeah. With the holidays coming around, we need all the help we can get. And if you recommended her, she has to be close to perfect."

I thought of Violet and grinned. "Well, I wouldn't say perfect."

"Soooo..." Lacey said clearing her throat meaningfully. "What did you and Magnus end up doing the other day? I know you snuck into the house pretty late."

I immediately turned away from her and looked out the window. I knew if I faced her, she'd be able to tell I wasn't being completely honest. "Oh, you know, we went back to his place and watched some of the old Brain Pain episodes."

"Yeah, the host, Jackie Cee, is so energetic. Don't you think? She's an amazing host."

"Definitely," I nodded. I had no idea who she was talking about. I hadn't watched long enough or paid enough attention to even know who the host was.

"And that co-host, Spike Kristoff, he's a riot... don't you think?"

I grunted a yes and pretended to be interested in what was going on outside. Of course, nothing was going on, so I just stared intently at various buildings that we passed on the way to work every day, hoping Lacey wouldn't notice that I was trying to dodge her questions.

She was silent, so I looked back at her and saw the wide smile on Lacey's face. That could only mean one thing: I was busted.

"Lesli, answer me honestly, did you spend your evening bumping uglies with Magnus? Because if you did, this is a judgment-free zone."

I sputtered. "What! What gave you that idea? Oh my gosh, Lacey. Get your head out of the gutter. I told you that we watched the show and that's all we did. For hours."

"Really? For hours?"

"Yep," I lied.

She continued to grin as if she'd caught me, but I wasn't going to confess anything. She didn't have concrete evidence. She was just guessing. "If you watched it for hours then you'd know there isn't a co-host. And the host is a he, not a she."

I opened my mouth to refute her statement, but it was clear that I had walked into her trap.

Lacey clapped her hands together in excitement, keeping the steering wheel straight with just her knees.

"Hands on the wheel, please," I muttered.

She placed her hands back on the wheel, but kept glancing at me from the corner of her eye. "Oh-em-gee. You got laid, didn't you? That's why you didn't show up at work yesterday, you were exhausted from all the dirty sex you were having with Magnus."

I covered my ears like a child and started humming. "Lalalalalalalalala."

Lacey was still carrying on as she pulled into a parking space in front of Ophelia's Angels. I was still yelling, "Lalalalalalalalala," at the top of my lungs like a crazy person, but desperate times called for desperate measures. I couldn't hear a word she was saying and I smiled at her smugly as she shook her head at me, when suddenly a loud knock sounded at our window. I looked up and to my surprise, Magnus stood there looking bemused.

Lacey stopped talking and I stopped humming.

"Are you ladies ok?"

I instantly remembered that my hands were over my ears. I lowered them, glowered at Lacey and slid out the car.

"We're fine. Move along," I said stiffly, sounding like a police officer. "There's nothing to see here."

I could hear Lacey giggling from the driver's seat. I

wanted to elbow her, but I wasn't close enough to do any damage. So disappointing.

"Ok then..." he said, backing up since I'd practically barked at him. "I guess I'll just move along then. See you inside."

I ignored him, but glanced at him as he walked away. The man had a perfect backside and I remembered exactly how it felt when I had my legs wrapped around it.

"I can't remember the last time I had sex," Lacey said unceremoniously as she got out the car. "Jude and I try sometimes but normally we both pass out during foreplay because we're so drained by the time we actually get to bed."

"Thanks for the information."

"You're welcome," she chirped.

We made our way to the front of the building with Lacey smiling like a Cheshire cat.

"And don't think that I didn't know you and Jude planned that whole kid invasion the other night."

"What? Us? Plan something so underhanded?" She pretended to look hurt. "Gosh, Lesli, your accusations are just plain malicious."

"Give me a break. You're a terrible actress."

Lacey smiled. "You're twenty-three. You're young, single, and cute. There's nothing wrong with doing what you want with whomever you want. There's nothing wrong with having a little fun."

Jude had certainly changed her. Lacey hadn't exactly been the type to throw caution to the wind before she met Jude. I liked this new aspect of my cousin's personality.

She opened the office door and I walked in. She followed closely behind me and continued talking. "You spent your formative years working your way through a rigorous and challenging program instead of making mistakes and dating losers like the rest of us. Just consider Florida a vacation from your rational self and old life. What happens in Florida, stays in Florida," she summed up in a stage whisper.

I laughed at her. She was right, but I was still determined to not admit to my little indiscretion with Magnus.

The other half of the guilty party in question was chatting with Maya at the water cooler. She was still on crutches and apparently had solicited Magnus's help.

"Gosh, this water is cold. It's just what I need considering how hot it just got in here," I heard Maya say flirtatiously.

I couldn't help myself, I laughed out loud and caught Magnus's attention as a result. We shared a little smile that made my heart seem to skip a beat. I flushed and looked elsewhere, almost running into an open door.

Jude appeared at the door and said, "Careful there, partner. Doors are expensive to replace."

I groaned and mumbled an apology, saying something about being clumsy.

"Your friend, Violet, I sent her an email. She's coming in for an interview in a few minutes."

"That's great! You'll like her. She's pretty cool."

"She sounded... umm…" He seemed to be pensive as he searched for the right word. "She sounded very enthusiastic, to say the least. Her direct quote was that she would 'work her ass off for me.'"

"Yikes," I said.

"She's a little rough around the edges, I take it?"

"That's a pretty diplomatic way to put it."

"Anyway, I'm looking forward to meeting her. I might have to make her memorize the employee handbook though since she's a little bit much."

"We have an employee handbook?"

Jude frowned and scratched his chin. "I've never actually seen it, but I think we have one of those." He turned to Lacey. "Babe, we do have an employee handbook, don't we?"

"No."

"Oh. I guess I should write one."

Lacey shook her head. "Pitiful." They exchanged a little smile with each other and I couldn't help but notice how much they genuinely liked each other. Their relationship was so easy-going, so natural. Yeah, they teased each other, but it was never nasty or mean-spirited. In the time I'd been living with them, it had become clear how much they enjoyed just being with each other. They were a perfect match and I found myself hoping maybe one day I would have what they had.

And as circumstances would have it, at that very moment my eyes connected with Magnus's. He was still stuck at the water cooler with a chatty Maya. He didn't smile. His eyes were hard to read as he studied me silently. I wondered what he was thinking. I was thinking if maybe fate was playing a role and maybe, just maybe, Magnus might be the one for me.

But there's no way I could be that lucky. A billionaire bachelor wouldn't be interested in a real relationship with me especially since I'd already slept with him, right? I sincerely doubted he'd ask me out again since he most likely got what he wanted.

I turned away, feeling uneasy under his gaze. I knew eventually I would have to talk to him, but eventually didn't have to be right now.

I walked into my office, booted up my computer and started working. A few hours passed and I realized I'd been in deep concentration when someone hissed my name.

I turned in the direction of my office door and Violet stood there. I barely recognized her. She had straightened her unruly blonde hair and pulled it back into a very neat bun. She was also wearing a smart, black pantsuit that looked sophisticated and professional. It was like seeing Violet all grown up.

"Hi," she said, waving at me. "I know you're working, but I just wanted to say hi."

"Hi," I said. "Are you on your way to the interview?"

"Actually, I just finished. I think it went well. Hopefully, I'll get the job."

"I'm sure you did great. I hope you get it too."

"Yeah. This place is great. Jude, Lacey, Aidan... Everyone who interviewed me has been amazing. You're so lucky to be related to such cool peeps. Anyway, I'll see you. Thanks so much for setting me up with this interview!"

"You're welcome," I said as she sashayed out.

I turned away from the door and was about to reach for my mouse when someone cleared their throat. I turned around and it was Magnus.

"Hi," he said. I tried not to think of how handsome he looked today. He was effortlessly virile and attractive, no matter what he wore... or didn't wear.

My mind instantly went back to the other night. I thought of how I felt wrapped in his arms.

"Hi," I said more curtly than I meant, but I didn't apologize. Instead, I immediately turned away and started returning emails. I hoped he wouldn't notice my skin flushing in his presence and my hands were shaky as I typed. His presence unsettled me before we'd slept together, but now after our rendezvous, I was a thousand times more unsettled by his nearness.

"Can we talk?" he asked, coming into the office and standing next to me. He dropped his voice so that only I could hear him. "I just want to make sure you're alright—"

"I'm fine."

"It's just that you left so abruptly... I figured you were upset about what happened between us?"

I just wanted him to shut up. I was too embarrassed to deal with my emotions, especially since I wasn't sure how I felt about anything. Apparently, he didn't get the hint. I was torn between being upset with him and wanting to hide from embarrassment.

"Nothing happened between us," I hissed.

He raised a brow and his voice dropped an octave, making it that much sexier. "I wouldn't say nothing."

I sighed and turned to face him. "Look. It was a mistake. I'm fine. I don't want to talk about it. I would rather just pretend it never happened. Like I said, it was a mistake. So if you don't mind, I'm working..." I gestured toward the computer. "If you'd excuse me..." I let my voice trail off and I expected him to say something else, but he didn't.

He just turned around and walked out without another word.

I instantly felt terrible. He didn't deserve to be yelled at because of my own insecurities, but I had reacted to his presence like a cornered rabid animal. God, I felt like such a jerk. But then I convinced myself I wasn't a jerk. I'd just been assertive. That night *had* been a mistake. And it was a mistake I wasn't interested in repeating, at least that's what I was telling myself.

I shook my head. I didn't know what I wanted. My adventure in Florida was turning out to be more of a misadventure and I didn't know what to do about it. I looked up from my computer and through the window which faced the parking lot.

I watched as Violet attempted to pull out of the parking lot and almost ran into Magnus who was walking to his car. She apologized profusely, and he shrugged it off, looking distracted. To my surprise, Violet got out of the car and started to flirtatiously dust him off, although he was clearly not dirty or injured in any way.

My eyes narrowed as she chatted with him. She touched his arm every now and then. I found myself leaning forward until my forehead was almost pressed against the window. She laughed at something he said and in response, he smiled a little. And then her cell phone was out and so was his.

"Are they seriously exchanging numbers?" I hissed to myself. They clearly were. I was seething on the inside.

I could see Violet smiling at him and she placed a hand on his sleeve and gave him another flirtatious smile before walking away. He watched her walk away and gave her a small wave before getting into his fancy car and zooming off.

I swallowed back the lump in my throat. I was jealous because in my mind Violet was moving in on my territory. And then I reminded myself that I wasn't interested in some womanizing billionaire.

But if that were true, why did my heart ache at the thought of Magnus seeing the one person that I considered a friend?

ranky didn't begin to describe how I was feeling as I stepped out of Lacey's car and prepared for a very, very long day at the studio.

"Have fun!" she yelled to me, and I waved at her but grunted in reply. I was in a terrible mood. I had barely gotten any sleep because every time I closed my eyes I dreamt about the evening Magnus and I had spent together, but instead of it being us making love, it was Magnus and Violet. Lacey had woken me up several times in the middle of the night to ask me what was wrong because apparently I'd been yelling at them in my sleep. That, in turn, had awoken baby Sebastian. I had apologized profusely to Lacey and had made it up to her by staying up all night with Sebastian until he fell back to sleep at four o'clock.

Now I was exhausted. It was six o'clock. I'd had at

most ten minutes of sleep before I needed to get back up to head out for the first taping of the Brain Pain episode.

I expected Lacey to be just as out of it as I was, but she had shrugged off the sleep interruption and had declared she was used to it.

I didn't want to do anything but sleep, I thought to myself, as I was escorted to the entrance of the studio by direction of a security guard who was way too chipper for my taste. I didn't know I was such a grumpy person without sleep. I was learning a lot about my true self, courtesy of Florida.

There was a flurry of activity and I didn't know where to go, so I just stood there wondering what to do and when to do it.

"Morning," a voice said behind me, and I instantly recognized Magnus's voice. He looked nice, dressed in faded gray jeans and a close-fitting black shirt.

He handed me a cup of coffee and I happily accepted it, avoiding his eyes. It had been tough avoiding him for the past two weeks, but I had succeeded. Too bad I didn't feel good about it.

"Thank you. Thank you so much." I was grateful. Caffeine was exactly what I needed.

"Ready for today?"

I shook my head. "I'm exhausted and not in the best of moods."

"Couldn't sleep? Nervous about the recording?"

I nodded. I didn't dare tell him about a certain X-rated dream that had really been the reason I couldn't sleep.

"Mr. Deacon?" interrupted a young man with uncertainty in his voice.

"Yes?"

"I'm Dale." Dale was a redhead with freckles. He was a little round and seemed to be under five feet tall. Surprisingly, his voice was quite deep which caught me off guard. "I'm your personal assistant while on set. I need to lead you to makeup. Please come with me."

"And what about Ms. Cabot?"

He looked unsure. "I don't know. I guess she can come too. All the VIPs have private suites. So if you would like to bring her, you can."

"Would you like to join us?" Magnus asked.

"No. I'll just wait here." I was delighted that I would have some breathing room. I didn't feel like I was up to the task of even talking to Magnus right now.

Dale nodded. "Sounds good. I'll send someone over to get you into makeup."

Dale led Magnus away when another person popped up next to me. "You're one of the contestants, right?"

Before I could answer, she grabbed me by the sleeve and started to lead me away. She looked like a little old lady, but she had a steel grip and I didn't even bother pulling away.

"I'm Celeste. We're going to get you all dolled up and then you'll be ready for action. How does that sound?"

"Sounds great."

"Excellent."

Ten minutes later I was "dolled up" as Celeste put it and positioned next to Magnus on set. I studied the other six contestants.

"Is that Ruben Mitchell?" I asked in disbelief.

"Who's Ruben Mitchell?" Magnus said.

I turned to Magnus with a look of incredulity on my face, "He's an Olympian. He brought home at least four gold medals last year. He's a competitive swimmer."

Magnus's face showed no sign of recognition. He just shrugged. And then I looked at the other contestants and instinctively grabbed Magnus's arm in excitement. "Oh my God, do you see that woman over there? With the blue shirt and dark jeans?"

"Uhh yeah… my arm." He grimaced.

I looked at him. "What?"

"You're killing my arm."

"Oops. Sorry," I said, letting go of him. "I'm just really excited. She's like one of my heroes."

"Oh really?" he said, finally showing some interest. He honestly looked bored and a little down. I wondered what all that was about. He was probably missing Violet, I thought before telling myself to stop being obsessive about something that was none of my business.

"She's a scientist. I took a class with her years ago as part of an exchange program. I was like sixteen at the time."

"Was she good?"

"Yes, she's amazing." I sighed. "She probably doesn't remember me. I'm sure she's had thousands of students."

"Maybe she does. You should go over and say hello."

I shook my head, feeling intimidated. "No. It was a long time ago and she has her own show on the Science Channel where she discusses everything from DNA to human sexuality. She's a genius." I frowned. "We're going to lose."

"Do you know who that guy is?" Magnus asked me. I looked in the direction of where he was pointing and saw a tall lanky dude, shooting daggers with his eyes. And those daggers were directed at Magnus.

I shook my head. "He doesn't look familiar."

"That's my former partner."

"Former? Is that why he's looking at you like he wants to step on your face and push you into an early grave?"

Magnus laughed so hard at my statement that others turned in our direction to see what was so funny. I couldn't help but laugh, too. I was pretty funny, I guess.

"He hates me. That's for sure. We parted ways at least five years ago and he started his own company which is swiftly becoming one of my chief competitors. He's doing well for himself."

"Oh man, did you fire him?"

"No… I gave him two choices and he chose the option to leave."

"So in other words, you fired him?"

"Kind of."

"Let's see… We have an Olympian, a scientist, and your sworn enemy as competitors. I think our chances of winning have just gone down to nil."

"No biggie. We can take them."

"You're way too confident."

"I don't know any other way to be. Ready to do this, partner?" He raised his hand to high-five me when someone shouted, "Magnus! Lesli! Over here!"

We looked in the direction of the voice to see Violet struggling to get away from not one, but two security guards.

"Can you tell these guys to let me go? They think I'm some sort of stalker."

"She's not allowed on the set," a security guard said to us.

"You're not allowed on the set," I echoed. What could I say? I was a rule follower.

"Fine, just fine. I'll cheer for you guys from the audience," she said, swatting at the security guard's hands. "Leave me alone. I know how to get to the audience side.

I do NOT need an escort." She looked back at me and said, "Good luck, Lesli! You got this, girl!" And to Magnus, she flirtatiously said, "See you tonight."

She flounced away while the security guards looked on shaking their heads. "We'll have to keep an eye on that one. She looks like trouble."

"So, you're seeing Violet tonight?"

"She's persistent," was all Magnus said.

I made a noncommittal sound, but inside I was fuming.

A photographer came by to take a picture of all the contestants and, for some reason, she said to us, "Don't you guys make a lovely couple."

"We're not a couple," I grumbled.

The photographer winced and mumbled an apology.

"What's going on with you today?" Magnus had the nerve to ask.

"Nothing. Absolutely nothing."

He looked at me funny and I ignored him. It had been a few weeks since Violet had interviewed and been hired by Jude. She was a great worker and fit in with the team instantly, especially Maya. But I was starting to hate her. It was official, she and Magnus were dating. She had told anyone in the office that would listen.

I knew I didn't have a right to hate her, after all, I'd had my chance with Magnus and I'd pushed him away. However, it pissed me off to no end that he liked her.

And it felt like Violet was betraying me by going out with him. But she didn't know that I liked him. In fact, I'd gone out my way to talk about how much I didn't like him. When Violet had mentioned it to me initially that she was going out with Magnus, she'd asked me if I was ok with it. I'd pretended that it was no big deal and had replied, "Have fun!"

But clearly, I was anything but ok. I was angry and had spent the entirety of last week villainizing Magnus and Violet in my head. I knew it was petty, but it was either that or acknowledge that I had feelings for Magnus and the idea of him going out with my best friend made me sick to my stomach.

I felt so stupid for being so conflicted. I knew I was being unfair to Violet who I was now keeping at arm's length. She'd looked hurt and had asked me if she had done anything wrong. I didn't have the heart to tell her that I didn't like that she was dating Magnus, nor did I want her to know that I was interested in him. So instead I'd given her the silent treatment every now and then. I felt so bad about my behavior. I knew I was being childish, but I was at a loss in terms of what it was that I should be doing.

I broke out of my reverie as the lights popped on and an announcement filled the air.

"It's time for Brain Pain," said our host with a beatific

smile. He was tall with beautiful hair, and sparkling blue eyes, I finally noticed.

"I'm Mickey Sims. Welcome to our show. Tonight, we have a special charity event for your viewing pleasure. The charity event will last for the next three weeks, so tune in each week for a new adventure where the competing celebrity and a representative from his or her charity compete to win one million dollars."

The crowd clapped and cheered as queued.

I rolled my eyes and Magnus looked at me with amusement. I knew I was being unnecessarily cranky, but whatever. He was dating Violet of all people.

"Just in case you're just tuning in, here's how this show will go. Each challenge will be about strength or smarts. Some challenges will be team challenges and some challenges will be done by one person."

He briefly explained which charities each of us were competing for and I begrudgingly acknowledged that each of the charities listed was reputable and supported a good cause. I wasn't very competitive, but knowing that if we lost, it would be to a good cause was enough to make me feel better.

There was the usual game show chitchat and then we were told to stand at our placemats, which had the words pain or brain situated on giant buttons on the floor.

"Teams, in front of you there are two large buttons. One is for pain and one is for brain. When I tell you, one person from the team will make a selection by stepping on either the button for pain or the button for brain. The catch is, that selection will not be for you, but for your partner's challenge... brain or pain. And the time to choose is now!"

Without hesitation, I jumped on a button, smiled broadly and said, "Pain."

Before Magnus could say a word, his position was locked in. He looked at me in shock and I smiled brightly at him. God, I didn't know I could be so bad. And it kind of felt good.

As luck would have it, all the other contestants chose Pain too. I guess we all had a personal vendetta against our partners.

The host looked absolutely delighted by our selections. Too delighted in my opinion. "Look behind you to find out what Brain Pain has in store for you today."

I happily turned around and as they pulled the curtains back, I saw it. There were four makeshift hills covered in dirt and standing about twelve feet high.

"This will be relatively easy," the host said. "You just climb that hill and ring the bell at the top. Easy peasy, right?" He gave us a big smile. "But you'll climb it dragging half your body weight."

I wasn't impressed yet. Magnus seemed like a strong guy. He could probably easily pull half his body weight.

The host smiled broadly again. "And did we mention these?"

Suddenly sprinklers came on and each hill slowly became a slippery mess.

"The game is easy. First contestant up the hill wins immunity."

I couldn't keep the gleeful smile from spreading across my face. I gave Magnus a thumbs up. "Good luck out there... partner."

He winced. "I'm going to get you back for this."

"Now who's cranky?"

I watched in glee as he was marched to the back to don his costume for the competition. He came out about ten minutes later with the rest of the contestants wearing bright purple jumpsuits and goggles.

I sat down with a bottle of water and prepared to watch the show and, boy, it was quite a show.

Each contestant started the race by standing in front of the hill. I noticed they all had utility belts attached to their waists. The utility belt had a rope attached to it and at the end of the ropes were sandbags. The sandbags were of various sizes, depending on each contestant's weight. I could see the tension in their shoulders as they waited for the bell to sound.

I was excited and more than a little relieved that Magnus was the lucky participant for this particular challenge.

The bell sounded and immediately Magnus scrambled toward the hill, dragging half his body weight as if it weren't the size of two toddlers. His sworn enemy was struggling to make it up his own hill and kept slipping and sliding.

"He's going to slip and fall before they even turn the water back on," I muttered.

And I was right. The lanky guy went sliding down the hill and landed face down on his own sandbag. I giggled.

The crowd was going wild now. It was just Magnus, the scientist, and the Olympian. I was sure the Olympian was going to win. And then they turned the sprinklers on.

Magnus and the Olympian went sliding back down the hill, covered in mud. Dr. Joseph made her way to the top and was just about to push the button that would give her the win when she lost her footing and went sliding down the hill.

Now it was anyone's game. The other three contestants were skinnier than Magnus. It wasn't that he was out of shape, but it was clearly hard to pull so much muscle up the hill, especially a steep wet hill.

Finally, all four contestants had regained their footing and were slowly dragging themselves up. They were covered in mud and I didn't know how they could even see anymore. Their bright purple jumpsuits were no longer bright or purple, but muddy and gross. Their goggles were covered in dirt and caked with mud. They all seemed to be moving remarkably slower than before.

The crowd was going wild though. It seemed the weaker the contestants became, the wilder the crowd was. I swear I could even hear Violet screeching.

And finally, the contestants were no longer neck and neck. Dr. Joseph was again toward the top, Magnus was about a foot away, as well. The Olympian and Magnus's enemy were still struggling with their footing and weren't gaining any ground.

With a heroic effort, Magnus hoisted himself up and was about to hit the button when he lost his footing and went tumbling down the hill. He slid on his back, straight down the hill, and landed with a plop in a puddle of mud. And at that very moment Dr. Joseph hit the button, winning the round and seizing the sprinklers.

I couldn't help but feel amused as the host went around and tried to interview each contestant. They were all out of breath and spent, leaning against their respective hill.

"That was so hard," the Olympian said. He then called up to Dr. Joseph, "You're amazing, Doctor."

The rest of the audience cheered and the host yelled up to her, "Come on down, Dr. Joseph. You've won your team immunity!"

With a whoop and a punch in the air, she gleefully slid down the hill and landed next to the host.

"How does it feel to win immunity and be one step closer to winning a million dollars for your favorite charity?"

"Amazing!" she shouted, and the audience cheered.

"We're going to get all cleaned up and then we'll be back after these messages."

And with that, they cut recording. Magnus's personal assistant, Dale, showed up and whisked him off. The other contestants were also taken away.

I was having a great time.

Then suddenly a production assistant was standing next to me. "Ma'am, it's time to get into costume."

"Excuse me?" I said.

"Your costume. It's time to get changed."

"But what's the challenge? We're doing another challenge?"

"Oh, I see you're not familiar with the format of the show."

"Ummm…yeah. I'm not."

"Well, Dr. Joseph's team won, so they don't have to do anything for this round. Your team, on the other hand, has to do another challenge."

"Another challenge?"

"Yep."

"Tell me it's a brain challenge."

She laughed. "Nope. Another pain challenge."

I groaned.

"Tell me I don't have to climb a hill covered in water and mud."

"You'll see," was the furtive answer I received.

Ten minutes later, I too had on a purple jumpsuit and goggles. I bit my lip waiting to hear what I had to do.

The host smiled. "Welcome back to a special charity episode of Brain Pain. Dr. Joseph and her partner have immunity and are guaranteed a spot in the last round. And who will join them? Will it be Ophelia's Angels? Dogs Are Love? Or Jesse's Children? We shall see. Contestants, to your starting places."

"Good luck," Magnus said, totally not meaning it. He had a wide smile on his face. It reminded me of my own smile while I had watched him.

I couldn't help myself. Like a child, I stuck my tongue out at him and he laughed.

Suddenly a spotlight came on on the far side of the studio, showing us our next challenge. Three inflatable slides were illuminated with black light and sitting at the base of each slide was a pool of neon green slime.

I wanted to say nope and just walk away, but I couldn't do that to Jude or Lacey. I had a mission to fulfill and I totally planned to go through with it. I squared my shoulders and took my place next to a ladder in front of a slide. The other contestants did the same.

"Contestants, you have three minutes to find several items that we've hidden in the slime. The game is simple. The first person to find the most items before time is up wins. And that time starts… NOW!"

I scrambled up the ladder and then worked my way to the slide. I slid down in a whoosh and then found myself submerged in nasty lime green, sticky, sticky slime. "This is sooooo gross," I groaned as the slime immediately stuck to my hair, my face, my entire jump-suit. I bobbed around, searching for anything solid. The audience cheered relentlessly and their encouraging words pushed me to try my hardest.

My hands found the first item and victoriously, I pulled it out of the slime and waded to the side of the pool to toss my item in the net hanging there.

And then I did it again and again, paying no atten-tion to the other contestants or the crowd as I searched as best as I could for another item. "Ten seconds," the host yelled.

I knew it was now or never. I had avoided diving under, but I desperately wanted to win this one for Ophelia's Angels. I took a deep breath, dove under, ignoring the feeling of claustrophobia that suddenly overwhelmed me while immersed in the thick slime. Before panic ensued, I grabbed frantically for something solid and, to my surprise, my hands closed over something the size of a grapefruit. Quickly, I came up for a breath and tossed the item, which I now recognized as a ball, into my net. And with that, the bell went off.

Breathless, I pulled at the goggles on my face and tried to wipe them off. It was no use. They were covered in slime. Every inch of me was, but at least without the goggles on, I could see around me. The host sent a team of assistants to count the items in each of our nets. I waited with my sticky fingers crossed. And I wasn't disappointed.

"And Ophelia's Angels wins. They're moving on to the final round!"

Suddenly, Magnus was there. His hands were on me pulling me out of the pool of slime and embracing me in a big hug.

I hugged him back, totally forgetting I was angry with him. And then suddenly I felt other arms wrapped around the both of us. Violet was hugging me and Magnus.

It was a giant group hug and I knew we looked ridiculous, but what the hell, I thought. How often was a girl hugged by her best friend and the man of her dreams all at once?

The thought gave me pause. Was Magnus the man of my dreams? If so, I'd thrown away my chances of being with him.

I reluctantly pulled myself out of his arms but Violet stayed holding on to Magnus. They were both covered in slime thanks to my disgustingness, but they didn't seem to mind.

The host was interviewing me. "Great job. How do you feel?"

"Accomplished."

The host's smile was genuine. "Well, you certainly accomplished a whole lot. We'll see you here tomorrow. Same time. Same place. Tune in for more Brain Pain when our finalists, Ophelia's Angels and the Cycle Psychos, will battle it out for the grand prize of one millionnnnnnn dollars!"

And suddenly that was a wrap. The host left without uttering another word.

I looked around, confused and then a production assistant appeared and handed me a towel. "Good job."

The other contestants congratulated me and I thanked them as I tried to rub the goo out of my hair.

"You were amazing out there," Violet said. "You both were." She turned to Magnus. "Sorry you lost, Magnus, but it's a good thing you had Lesli to make up for your shortcomings."

"Thanks for that, Violet."

"Sure, no problem."

I couldn't help but laugh.

And then the production assistants were around us.

"Feel free to get changed and we'll see you guys in a week. Congrats!"

Violet hooked her arm around Magnus's and then slowly pulled it away. It was covered in slime, courtesy of me.

"I'll meet you outside, while you get cleaned up," she said, wiping her hands on her lap trying not to look disgusted.

I walked toward our dressing rooms and Magnus trailed behind me.

"Why are you following me? Don't you have things to do with Violet?" I tried to keep my tone light, but I couldn't.

He maneuvered himself in front of me and said, "What's with all the attitude lately? Did I do something to upset you?" He looked down at me and I had to resist the urge to reach out and touch him. I wanted to do nothing else but that. He was so close. Close enough to kiss. I reprimanded myself for even allowing myself to think about him that way. He was Violet's, not mine.

"I don't know what you're talking about." I quickly dodged him and kept walking. With a few strides, he easily caught up with me.

"If we're going to be working together, the least you could do is be civil toward me."

"I am civil!" I yelled in a very uncivil-like manner.

"You've been short with me. You've made snide

comments AND you chose pain without even consulting me."

I snickered. "Well, that is the name of the game, Magnus. I was just playing the game."

"At my expense."

"Hey, I had to do pain too."

"Yeah, but you didn't know that when you selected pain for me."

"You're being too sensitive. I was just playing the game and I suggest you do the same."

"That's hard to do when my partner has a personal vendetta against me. I thought I had to worry about the other contestants, but no, the person out to get me is the one person who should be supporting me."

"Stop with the accusations. It's all in your head. I'm not out to get you. What reason would I have to be out to get you?"

"I have no idea and you won't talk to me long enough for me to find out. You haven't really talked to me since that night we—"

I instantly turned around and hushed him. "I don't want to talk about that. And why does what happened between us that night even matter? You moved on quickly. And to add insult to injury, you moved on to the one person in this world I consider a friend."

He instantly became defensive. "Why do you care who I date? You didn't want to date me, remember?"

"I don't care who you date. I don't care about you at all. You just have some nerve to date one of my friends."

"I didn't know she was your friend when I met her."

"Well, you found out eventually."

"And when I found out, I tried to ask you how you felt about it and you told me you didn't care. Remember that?" I thought back to the texts I'd received from him when he'd started dating Violet, which I had pointedly ignored and then responded with, "It's none of my business." God, I had been really abrupt with him, yet still blamed him for everything. My anger was irrational and misplaced, but I didn't care.

"I mean, yeah. I don't care who you date. It's just a matter of decency." There wasn't much conviction in my tone. I didn't even believe me.

"Quit with the lame excuses. Either you care or you don't. Being wishy washy doesn't suit you."

"And being an arrogant jerk definitely suits you."

"Me? I'm the jerk? You think I'm the one with the problem?"

"Clearly."

"I thought you were different. I thought you were logical and reasonable."

For some reason, those words stunned. "I'm both those things, but that doesn't excuse you from doing something hurtful."

"Oh, so now we're finally getting somewhere. Me dating someone else is hurtful?"

"What? No. That's not what I meant at all."

"So what did you mean?"

I sighed in defeat. I didn't know what I was saying. I didn't know what I was thinking. I didn't know what I wanted. Actually, I did know what I wanted but I didn't know what to do since now I couldn't have it.

I wanted Magnus's attention. I wanted to date him, spend time with him. He should have been going out with me. Not Violet. Never Violet. Didn't he see that? I felt like the ugly, geeky friend. I felt insecure again. The makeover hadn't helped. Deep down inside I was still that teenage girl, unsure of herself, trying to live up to everyone's expectations without knowing what her expectations were for herself.

I couldn't tell Magnus what I wanted because I didn't even know what I wanted.

I was a mess. I had to figure me out, but in the meantime, I needed someone to blame for my misery and that someone had been Magnus. He didn't deserve that. He'd been nothing but gentlemanly and kind to me. It wasn't his fault that I was going through some sort of crisis. And it wasn't his fault that in the middle of getting to know myself, I had fallen head over heels in love with him.

I felt the tension ease from my shoulders as I allowed

those words to sink in. I was in love with Magnus and for some reason, being in love with him was bringing out the worst in me. Who was I kidding? That wasn't Magnus's fault. I just didn't know how to deal with this new feeling, this new emotion. I'd never been in love. And instead of being open to it and allowing Magnus to have a place in my life, I'd pushed him away. Our current situation was my doing. All of it. And it was about time I started taking accountability for it. It was time I grew up and stopped acting like a petulant child.

But where did I start? I'd been pretty horrible to him. I took a deep breath and just said what was in my heart. Well, not all of it. I wasn't ready for all of it yet. "Listen, I like you a lot, Magnus. And I respect you. I'm sorry that I've made things difficult between us for the past couple of weeks."

Magnus's shoulders instantly lost their tension too and his expression softened.

"I like you a lot, too. And it was never my intention to hurt you."

I nodded. "I understand that."

"So maybe we can work on being friends?"

I didn't want to be just his friend though. I knew that for sure. But friendship was what he was offering. So I would take it.

"I would like that," I said softly.

"Great."

We stood there just staring at each other, neither of us knowing what to say from there. The chemistry between us was unmistakable and yet, at least on my end, there was nothing I could do about it.

I looked away first. "I'm going to go scrub off all this slime."

"That's a good idea." His voice was soft and his eyes clearly said he wanted to say more but wasn't going to.

There was a little bit of mud, I realized, right below his ear. I reached out and attempted to dust it off when he caught my hand in his.

"Lesli, I—"

"You guys are still here? Better get a move on. We're set to start filming the next group," said one of the production assistants.

"Sorry. I'm just heading that way..." my voice trailed off and I realized that Magnus was still holding my hand.

I tugged my hand away from his slowly.

"I'll see you," I said, and then with a voice that didn't hide my regret, I added, "You shouldn't keep Violet waiting. She's not the most patient person."

He nodded and smiled a little although he looked lost in thought. "You're right about that."

He turned and I watched him walk away as the production assistant whisked me away.

"Hey, Lesli," he called to me, turning back again.

"Yeah?"

"I..." he shook his head and tried again. "I—I'll call you."

I smiled, knowing that he wanted to say much more. "I'll answer."

He turned away then and walked toward the studio exit and I sighed deeply. I didn't know love was so complicated, but then again, it probably hadn't needed to be. I'd messed up. And now I didn't know how to fix it. And even if I did fix it, I'd end up hurting a friend in the process. Feeling defeated, I let the busybody production assistant escort me to the dressing room. I could wash off the ickiness of the day, but unfortunately, getting rid of the icky emotions I was feeling wasn't going to be as easy.

11

"I can't believe I'm wearing these," Emmaline said as she pulled on the edges of her shorts. They were super short. I was surprised that her butt managed to stay in them.

"They're hot pants. They're supposed to be short," Misha responded as she shifted uncomfortably in her shoes.

"I feel like my privates can't breathe."

"They're not supposed to feel comfortable," Misha said again, "They're supposed to be sexy. Stop complaining."

Misha then started yanking at the fabric of her dress which kept riding up her thighs. "This stupid dress won't stay down."

"Oh, so it's alright for you to complain, but not me. Point taken," Emmaline said as she fought with her shorts.

"Ladies, ladies, let's not fight," Lacey said, stepping around the car. We all looked at her and couldn't help but laugh. Ever since she had shown up dressed like a member of the Bee Gees from the seventies, we couldn't keep it together.

She had on a curly blonde wig, tight bell-bottom pants and a shiny, blue metallic shirt. She was also about six inches taller since she was wearing platform heels.

"My feet already hurt," she complained. "You guys are lucky you're wearing go-go boots."

"Yes, I'm lucky that my feet are covered, but my butt might fall out any time."

"Well, if it falls out, I'll tell you," Lacey said, clearly tired of the complaining.

Emmaline was Lacey's other best friend whom she'd met in college. Emmaline, Misha, and Lacey were a dynamic trio and closer than most sisters I knew.

I adored them and seeing them all bicker with each other brought back fond memories.

"It would be a fun break from the kids, you'd said," complained Misha.

"It's going to be so fun, you'd said," complained Emmaline.

"And instead we look like very old and very unsuccessful prostitutes," finished Misha, finally giving up on tugging her skirt down. I directed my eyes away. She was dangerously close to flashing everyone.

Lacey tossed her hands up. "Well, this is what happens when you don't go with me to pick out your costumes. I gave you guys a chance and you were all like, 'Just pick whatever, Lacey,'" she said in a whiny tone. "So I picked whatever."

"As punishment—" Misha said.

"You know, I don't like your tone. I'm giving all of you a break from suburbia and this is how you thank me?"

"I thought you were going to get me a fairy costume?" Emmaline whined.

"Yeah, and I thought I was going to be Gene Simmons from Kiss," Misha said, folding her arms over her chest, which made her dress rise a tiny bit more. Yep, she was wearing polka dot panties, and by the end of the night everyone in the building would know it.

"You guys. It's a seventies themed party. None of those costumes would have made sense."

There was more grumbling of unhappiness when suddenly Lacey stomped her foot, making me laugh, and said, "Listen, we're not here for us. We're here to provide some moral support. Ok. Is that clear?"

Emmaline, Misha, and I looked at each other and then back at Lacey. "What are you talking about? Moral support for who?"

Lacey pointed at me. "For Lesli. Do you guys just tune out when I talk or something? I mean this is ridiculous."

"What? Why do I need moral support? What are you even talking about?" I was totally caught off guard. I felt like I spent nearly every day since leaving West Virginia caught off guard in some way or form.

"Because your best friend, you know, Violet, is dating your man!" Lacey said in disbelief as if she couldn't understand why I wasn't more upset.

"What?" Misha growled. She looked ready to fight someone.

"Seriously? What kind of friend is she?" Emmaline added. "Stealing your man!"

"I never trusted Violet, what a bi—" Misha didn't even know Violet.

I put my hands in the air and cut off Misha before she could continue. "Don't say it. Because she's not a you-know-what. She asked me if I would mind if she dated Magnus and I don't. I really, really don't. I mean, I didn't at the time. But whatever, it's my own fault. So all this—" I began gesturing to the three of them in costume. "Is unnecessary. I'm fine. The situation is under control, ok? It's fine."

"She's in denial," Emmaline said, shaking her head.

"I'm not in denial," I protested.

"No. You are, but don't worry," Lacey said, looking at me as if she pitied me. "We're all here for you."

I shook my head. "Seriously guys, I'm fine."

But I wasn't fine. I was far from it. I wasn't ok with Violet dating Magnus or Magnus dating Violet. I was just pretending that I was when actually it tore me up inside.

I thought being on friendly terms with Magnus would make the hurt go away, but it hadn't. As I'd promised that day after our first Brain Pain challenge, I'd answered his call. And every day for the past week, we'd talked. Some days we talked so long, I fell asleep on the phone. We were behaving like infatuated teenagers, talking to each other until the break of dawn most evenings. It would have been romantic if it weren't for the fact our conversations never strayed to that zone. We were strictly friends and I was careful to keep it that way. After all, Magnus was still dating Violet. I didn't want to betray my friend even though I sort of was by having an emotional affair with the man she was dating.

But just talking to Magnus made me feel more alive than anything else. We talked about the most ridiculous subjects and I learned so much about him. We talked about aliens and pseudo-anthropology. We talked about old sci-fi TV shows and our favorite characters. For two people who'd grown up in two very different worlds, we had a lot in common. And I felt it was fate that we met.

Which was silly, because I didn't believe in fate until I'd realized I was in love with Magnus.

"You're too good for Magnus anyway. His loss, not yours," Lacey said suddenly.

"Really? A few weeks ago you were saying he was such a good catch."

"I'm running on two hours of sleep most days, so just ignore everything I say." Lacey turned to the others. "Ok. It's time to put Operation Magnus into action."

There were a few half-hearted cheers from Emmaline and Misha who were still trying to adjust their clothing but to no effect. The costumes were garish and there was no getting around it.

"You guys..." Lacey said, her voice dropping in warning that she was getting angry.

"What?"

"Operation Magnus," she snapped.

"What's Operation Magnus? I thought this was just a girls' night out."

"Yeah, I just wanted to eat ice cream at your place and watch Netflix uninterrupted."

"We're supposed to infiltrate the party, find Magnus, tell him he's making a big mistake, and then lock Violet out of the room so Magnus and Lesli can reconcile."

"What? That's a terrible plan." Misha was the abrupt one. She always spoke her mind. I think it was the tough city girl upbringing that made her that way.

Emmaline, the ever-practical friend, shook her head. "You've been watching too many romantic comedies."

"What? No, I haven't. I mean... they're on late at night when I'm up with the baby..." She paused and said, "Oh God, look at us. You're right. I think I saw this in a romantic comedy. I'm officially losing my mind."

Lacey looked sadly down at her outfit.

"Yes, you're totally losing your mind," Misha said. "But let's not ruin the night. Erik is home with the kids tonight so I'm making the most of it. I might actually have a few drinks."

"Me too," Emmaline said, finally leaving her shorts alone.

"But first ladies, I need some jeans... I can't flash people all night. I do have some standards."

"I have a pair of sweats in the backseat. Hold on."

Lacey started rummaging through her backseat, tossing various baby items out of the way as she did. With much fanfare, she pulled the sweatpants from the back of her car. "Ta-da!"

"You're the best," Misha said, snatching them from her hands. She put them on quickly and I couldn't help but laugh.

"Nice look... It has that whole stay-at-home mom meets—"

"1970s prostitute?"

We all began to laugh and I was happy for the lighthearted moment until a limousine pulled up to the curb. I instantly recognized who it belonged to. After all, there was only one like it in the country, maybe the world, even.

The driver came around and opened the door as we all watched. As I figured, Violet stumbled out in go-go boots, white hot pants and a cropped sheer, white top. She saw us and gave us a wave and started approaching us. She looked fantastic, of course. I looked like Velma from Scooby Doo in comparison.

"Love the costumes, ladies," she said. She frowned when she saw Misha. "What's up with the sweatpants? Get rid of them and show some legs."

"No, thanks. I don't want to catch a cold or something."

Violet laughed. "That's something my grandma would say. No offense—"

"No offense taken," Misha said with a tight smile. I was surprised Misha was able to control herself. Clearly, she was offended by Violet's comment, but she'd managed to restrain herself. Having children had apparently mellowed her.

I noticed then that Magnus didn't get out.

"Didn't Magnus come with you?" I asked, unable to help myself.

"Oh, he's showing up later. He had some business to take care of. He's kind of a bore. Always working. I thought dating a billionaire would be much more exciting, but it's been pretty much boredom after boredom. I had to practically beg him to come to this party." She shook her head. "Sad, isn't it?"

"Tragic," I muttered.

"Anyway, let's go get this party started! Wooohooo!"

We cheered too, with about a quarter of her enthusiasm, and then headed up the steps into the community center where the party was being held. It was a party held every year by a nonprofit who provided leadership training to other nonprofits in the city. Every year, various nonprofits in the area gathered for the party. It was the perfect networking event and the shindig attracted quite a few newscasters and famous people. Apparently, everyone wanted to be seen giving back to a good cause. Tickets weren't cheap. All employees for the nonprofits got in free, but everyone else paid a whopping $100 per plate. The proceeds were then awarded by a vote to the nonprofit deemed most deserving. I hoped Ophelia's Angels won, but I was biased. I loved working there.

The music was loud and pumping. To my surprise, there were already people on the dance floor, busting moves to seventies hits. Maya was there in full seventies dress, complete with crutches, and she instantly pulled me on the dance floor as soon as she saw me. She started dancing around me, yelling out, "Go, Lesli! Gom Lesli!

Go, go, go, Lesli!" And soon a circle had formed around us with other people cheering me on. I looked to Lacey, Emmaline, or Misha to save me, but they were all at the bar. Then Violet joined us and the three of us jiggled and wiggled around. I found myself laughing and actually having a good time.

I thought about how just a few weeks ago, I probably would have run from the dance floor, but now I was busting a move, badly, but I was having fun. Finally, the song ended. Maya high-fived me and went off with Violet to get a drink.

"Tearing up this dance floor has got me crazy thirsty," Maya said and Violet concurred. As I'd known they would, they'd gotten along instantly. They were so much alike, it was either they would get along great or hate each other. I was glad it was the former and not the latter.

As they walked away, I looked around, wondering if Magnus was there yet. From my position on the dance floor, I could easily see the entrance and exits. Magnus and I hadn't discussed the party the other day on the phone. We had just talked about his family and how his parents were finally reconciling after over a decade of not even speaking with each other. I was happy for him and wondered if it were family business or actual business that was making him run late today.

I tried to focus on the party instead of Magnus's

appearance. There were a ton of older people there, shaking it to music I hadn't heard since my youth. Mom had been a huge fan of music from the seventies. I was glad so many members of the community had shown up to support such a great cause.

I slinked away toward the side of the room as the dance floor began to fill up again. It was then that I saw him, and he instantly saw me too.

He made a beeline straight across the dance floor, smiling as he headed toward me. A couple twirling to a song being played by the DJ ran into Magnus, but he seemed to barely notice as he made his way to me. I watched him watching me. My whole body responded to his presence. I shyly looked his way as goosebumps appeared on my bare arms.

Finally, he was standing in front of me and I wanted to wrap myself in his arms in greeting. It took every fiber of my being not to.

"Hi."

"Hi."

"I—"

"You—"

We both started talking at the same time and then laughed. "You first," I said, still smiling. He looked so handsome even though he was wearing a white leisure suit that looked like something John Travolta wore in Saturday Night Fever. The movie had come out way before my time, but my mother loved John Travolta so I'd been commanded to watch all of his movies.

"You look great," he said to me. He then let his eyes scan my body. It was brief and discrete, but enough to make me feel flushed. I was wearing hot pants too and a cropped top. Thankfully, my shorts actually covered my bottom.

I blushed and said, "You look very John Travolta-ish."

He raised a brow and said, "Thanks. I think."

"You just look... gorgeous. The seventies suits you."

"The clothes, not the era," I said. I couldn't help myself. I was a history major after all.

"So do you want me to get you a drink or something?"

"Or something," I said facetiously. And then without thinking I reached my hand out to his and he took it. At that very moment, I saw Violet coming toward us. I guiltily removed my hand from his and opened my mouth to apologize. I know she saw us, but she seemed unconcerned as she made her way to us.

"Magnus! There you are! Come on, Channel Seven is here. Let's get a picture. I'll bring him right back, Lesli. I promise." And just like that, Violet whisked him off.

I wondered about her last comment, about bringing him back to me. Did she know that I was secretly interested in him? Or maybe it wasn't all that secret. She did just catch me holding hands with him. I didn't know what I'd been thinking. The only excuse I could give myself was that it was becoming harder and harder to keep my feelings in check when Magnus was around. I didn't know what to do from here, but I decided then and there to stop being afraid of how I felt. I vowed to tell Magnus by the end of the evening how I felt and I'd also have to tell Violet. My shoulders filled with tension again and my stomach did somersaults at the idea of how my words would hurt her, but I knew I couldn't hold it in any longer. I couldn't hide how I really felt from the world, not to mention from a friend.

I caught up with Misha, Emmaline, and Lacey. They'd been staring in my direction and when I approached, they tried to appear nonchalant. They didn't say a word but their silence spoke volumes.

"What?" I said with a hint of annoyance.

"You and Magnus seemed awfully cozy until Violet showed up."

"We're just friends."

"Friends don't stare into each other's eyes and hold hands," Emmaline said matter-of-factly as she helped herself to another flute of champagne as a waiter made his rounds.

I followed her lead and helped myself to one too. I needed a little liquid courage for what I planned to do tonight.

And then I thought to myself, maybe I needed to practice saying it out loud.

"You guys," I said taking a deep breath. "I'm in love with Magnus."

"I knew it," Lacey said.

"You need to tell him," Emmaline immediately added to the conversation. "From what Lacey's told us, he just started dating Violet, but you don't want things to progress too far along before telling him how you feel."

"So true," Misha said nodding. "Tell him how you feel and then rip his clothes off and have dirty sex with him in his limo. It's what I would do."

I giggled. "I'll definitely consider it."

"You do that," she agreed before waving to someone behind us. "Oliver and Grandma are here!"

"He made it," Lacey said as we moved as a group toward them. On his arm was Kat, Misha's grandmother.

We all hugged and fussed over each other.

"Welcome back! How was the vacation?" I asked.

"Great. Wonderful," Kat said.

"But I was ready to come home," Oliver said. "This old body isn't what it used to be. Kat, here," he said kissing her forehead. "Now, she could have stayed in Greece. You should have seen her, dancing on tables in the Greek isles."

Kat laughed. "I had a grand time. But I missed my apartment."

Oliver sighed. "I took her to the fanciest hotels money could buy, but this one wanted to experience hostels. I stayed at a hostel for this woman. I had to share a bathroom with strangers. It was almost inhumane." His tone was incredulous, which made the rest of us laugh.

Kat pinched the tip of his nose, in a very cute, affectionate manner, and said, "Oh, hush. You loved every minute of it."

"Only because I was with you..."

"You're too sweet." They shared a brief kiss.

"Ok, ok, get a room," Misha said, making a face.

"I might be your grandma but I'm also a sensual, hot-blooded woman with needs—"

Misha held her hands up and said, "Alright, alright. I get it. Ok. Cool. Whatever. Let's change the subject. Lesli's in love with Magnus."

I opened my mouth, closed it and then opened it again. "Thanks for telling the world, Misha."

"I knew love was in the air!" Oliver said giddily. "I'm so happy for you. Magnus is a great guy. Hard worker. You know he single-handedly rebuilt his family's wealth. His mom, Jenny, gave away the entire family fortune to some charlatan in Sri Lanka, I think it was." He shrugged. "But Magnus didn't feel entitled to her wealth like his father did. He couldn't have cared less, but his dad was always looking for a handout. I sort of got the feeling that's why he married Jenny. They never really had much in common. Anyway, Magnus made it his mission to build back the family fortune. Been working hard at it for nearly a decade. I have nothing but good things to say about him. You chose a real winner, Lesli."

I knew he was right. Magnus was a great guy. I wouldn't have fallen for him if he wasn't.

"So are you guys going to tie the knot?" Oliver asked.

"Woah, hold on Oliver," Lacey said. "He doesn't even know how she feels yet."

He looked at me in confusion. "But why?"

"It's a long story, Oliver, and he kind of has a girlfriend—"

"What?" Now he was frowning.

I filled them all in, leaving out any X-rated parts.

"Wow, the situation does sound pretty complicated," Kat said, looking concerned.

"It is." I felt forlorn suddenly. Why had I let things spiral out of control? If I hadn't been so stubborn and insecure, my relationship with Magnus would have progressed like all other normal people, but nooo, I had to make things difficult.

I was trying to find something to say when suddenly

the music came to a sudden stop and we all turned in the direction of the DJ who was looking a little bit afraid. Standing next to him, waving a microphone threateningly at the security guards was a familiar looking man. I just couldn't place him. He was young, tall, blonde.

And then it hit me. "That's Violet's boyfriend!"

"Violet's dating Magnus and has a boyfriend. How does she find the time?" Kat wondered out loud.

"I mean ex. That's her ex-boyfriend."

"What's he doing here? And why is he fighting the security guard over the microphone?"

"Leave me alone. I have something to say and I'm going to say it," Violet's ex-boyfriend shouted into the mike.

The security guards grabbed him and he ducked around them, disappearing under the table with the mike.

"Violet, sweetie," he said while kicking at the security guards' hands as they dragged him from underneath the table. "I only want to be with you!" he crooned.

I looked around for Violet who was standing there in shock. Magnus was by her side looking bewildered. The others and I moved closer, not wanting to miss a moment of this show.

The security guards now had Violet's ex-boyfriend by his underarms and were trying to drag him out.

"Oh wait, wait. Don't hurt him. He's the love of my life!"

There was an audible gasp from the audience, myself included. Magnus continued to look bewildered, turning from Violet's ex-boyfriend to Violet.

With much fanfare, Violet reached up and kissed Magnus on the cheek. "You're great. You really are but, you know, I just don't really feel anything between us."

Magnus opened his mouth to say something when Violet pressed her finger against his lips and said, "Shhh. Don't say anything. I know you're in shock. I know you'll never meet anyone else like me in your entire life and I'm sorry for you about that." She stood back and took his hands, continuing, "But trust me that I'll always have a special place in my heart for you. And you can always follow me on Instagram."

She happily reached for her ex-boyfriend's hand who took one last parting jab at Magnus. "Yo' man, you better not follow my girl on Instagram, got that?"

Violet giggled. "Oh, Steve. You're so virile and protective. I always loved that about you."

"Anything for you, girl. You know you're my girl, right? I love you so much. I messed up. I'll never kiss another woman again unless that other woman is you." His eyes were red as he started to tear up and his lips trembled.

"I love you, too," Violet said as her eyes began to

water. That was the end of the sweetness as they started slobbering on each other while the rest of us watched in shock.

"Get a room," someone shouted. I was pretty sure that someone was Misha.

"Let's get married. Haven't you always wanted to visit Vegas?" Steve said.

To everyone's surprise, Violet balked. "Slow down, buddy. I'm young and fun. I'm not going to let marriage ruin what I have left of my twenties. Are you freaking kidding me?"

Steve actually looked relieved. "Cool. Want to go get some noodles? There's this Vietnamese noodle place out near downtown. They let me park my camper there."

"You brought your camper with you?" she said, unwinding her arms from his neck and stepping back. "That's so gross. I always hated that camper."

They walked away arguing while the rest of us looked on.

"Well, that was something," Emmaline muttered.

"God, how embarrassing," Misha said as she helped herself to the pile of shrimp at the buffet table. "These are delicious."

Oliver popped up next to me with Kat by his side. "Here's your chance, Lesli. He's sad and single. Get ready to pounce."

I looked at Oliver and shook my head. No, I couldn't.

This couldn't be the right time to tell him. He'd just been publicly dumped.

"He's right," Kat said. "He's ripe for the picking... All vulnerable and sad."

I wanted to cover my ears and hide when suddenly Magnus walked in our direction. During Violet's speech his face had registered shock, then disbelief and then finally amusement. He didn't look amused now, he looked determined.

"Shhh... he's coming this way... he's coming this way," Lacey murmured. "Quick everyone, Pretend we weren't talking about him."

To my embarrassment, everyone started fake laughing and awkwardly talking about the weather.

Oliver was the worst offender. "Oh, Magnus. We didn't see you there." He patted him on the back with a hard hit. "Don't worry about the breakup. Things will turn around. We've all had our share of public humiliation."

Misha laughed and then quickly tried to cover it as a cough.

Magnus winced. "Yeah. That was pretty bad. I think I'm going to head out and lick my wounds."

"Nonsense. Stay. We're all friends here. No one's going to bring up the fact that you got dumped so publicly."

"No," Magnus said with a sigh, "I think I'll head out.

I've given the papers enough to talk about for one night." He looked at me then and I couldn't read the expression in his eyes as he said, "Goodnight, Lesli."

He turned to walk away and people cleared a path for him. Most were still whispering among themselves about the commotion Steve had caused.

I watched him walk away until he disappeared. My heart went out to him, but Oliver and Kat were right. Maybe this was my moment. I looked at Lacey and said, "Don't wait up for me."

I could hear cheers behind me and knew Oliver, Lacey, and the rest of the gang were cheering me on.

I picked up the pace, racing through the crowd and down the stairs. People looked at me curiously, but I knew it was now or never. I had to tell him how I felt or at the very least I had to show him.

"Hey," I called as I closed the distance between us.

He turned around and looked confused but pleased to see me.

I swallowed hard, "I could say that I'm sorry about what happened, but I'm not sorry at all." I surprised myself by my own bluntness.

"I don't know what you want me to say." He looked confused and on guard.

"I don't know what I want you to say either, but I do know that I'm glad that it's over between you and Violet. She wasn't right for you."

He looked at me quizzically, "Really? Then who is?"

I raised my hand and he gave a gruff laugh.

"You?"

I nodded and gave him a partial smile. "I think, just maybe, that I might be."

He stared at me and didn't say a word and then he took my hand and pulled me into the limo with him. I knew I should have waited, but I couldn't. I had already waited too long in my opinion.

I unzipped his pants as soon as the limo door closed and he spread his legs, allowing me better access. I got down on my knees and pulled his already straining sex into my mouth. I wanted this. I wanted to taste him. I wanted to claim what I felt was rightfully mine.

I sucked at the tip and he shifted, trying to maintain his cool. I looked up at him and he looked down at me as I pulled not just the tip but the rest of him deep into my mouth.

He groaned then and grabbed my head. He kept my face to his cock as I moved it in and out of my mouth, adjusting the speed of my licks and teasing him with my tongue. I used my other hand to play with his balls and I didn't know it was possible, but he stiffened even more, getting harder and longer.

I couldn't wait, I needed him right then and there. I didn't care that the driver might hear us. I climbed into Magnus's lap and he pulled my shorts off and pushed my panties to the side. He began to finger me as he kissed me all over, planting kisses along the tops of my breasts and freeing my nipples with a sense of urgency, sighing as he sucked one and then the other into his mouth. I ran my fingers through his hair and moaned.

And then as I did, he fingered me harder, pushing one finger and then another deep into me. I gasped and begged him.

"Put it in," I whispered against his ear.

"Say please," he teased.

I decided to take matters into my own hand. I grabbed his length and lowered myself on it. I wanted to take him all in at one time, but it had been a while since our last encounter so I had to take my time.

But that made it even more pleasurable. I slowly took him in inch by inch and he tossed his head back and let me control the rhythm of our lovemaking as I buried him in my wetness.

I began to move up and down, almost letting the tip of his sex exit my center before settling back down. He took over then, unable to control himself, and began speeding up the rhythm of our lovemaking.

"God, you feel good..." he moaned, his head still tossed back.

I couldn't respond, I was on the point of no return. An orgasm hit me and I closed my eyes and luxuriated in the feel of it. I couldn't breathe. I couldn't think. My whole body tensed, and with a gasp, I collapsed forward as my inner muscles shook, clenching around Magnus's still hard cock.

He grabbed my waist then and easily bounced me up and down, penetrating me as deeply as he could in our current position, as my head lay against his shoulder, until he too found his sweet spot and finally, with one last thrust of his hips, he came inside of me.

I didn't stir. I sat there with him still buried in me as the limo continued to move toward what I assumed was his home.

He began to rub my back and he kissed my neck.

"That was…"

I put a finger up to shush him. "Don't talk. You'll ruin the moment."

"Yes, ma'am," was all he said, and I smiled. He wrapped his arms around and me and said, "So does this mean you're spending the night?"

"If you'll have me."

"I can't imagine anything better."

He surprised me then by tilting my head up. "This time… I would like to wake up next to you. Deal?"

I shrugged. "We'll see."

He frowned. "You know, I do have some handcuffs somewhere. I can handcuff you to the bed."

I was feeling wanton. "Oh really? Kinky."

He squeezed my bare behind. "Seriously. Tell me that you'll stay."

Something about his voice was vulnerable and his eyes held an emotion that I wasn't ready to identify.

I buried my head in his neck and said, "I'll stay."

He wrapped his arms around me. I was cognizant of the fact that he was getting hard again and I was getting wet again.

I kissed him long and hard. "Round two?" I said as I began moving my hips.

"Yes, please," was all he said as I slowly began again to make love to him.

The next morning, the spray of the shower cascaded down my back and front. I couldn't help but think yet again how fancy Magnus's shower was. There were shower heads positioned strategically on several walls which meant no matter where I turned, the warmth of the water caressed my body. His shower was pure luxury and I loved every minute of it.

Seconds later, Magnus peaked in. "Care if I join you?"

I don't know why I felt shy, but I did. We'd spent the entire night making love. I'd let him do things to me that I'd never done with another man, things I'd only read about but never experienced. I'd done all those things plus more with Magnus. But under the moonlight, it hadn't been any big deal. It was almost as if nothing at night was real, but in the harsh judging light of the day, I felt differently. I felt exposed.

Maybe I was some sort of sex werewolf, I thought nonsensically. I turned into a wanton, sex goddess at night, but was a prude in the light of day.

Trying to sound confident but failing, I said, "Sure."

He stepped in with me and I tried to ignore his cock, which was partially erect and getting harder by the minute.

He stepped up behind me and gathered some soap in his hand.

"Do you want me to wash your back?"

"Sure."

Apparently, my morning vocabulary was limited to just saying sure.

His warm hands slid across my shoulders and I sighed.

"God, your hands feel good."

He chuckled and when he was done he pulled me back into his arms and just held me. I knew I should have been comfortable and felt relaxed, but for some reason I was tense.

As if noticing, he let me go and said, "Is something wrong?"

"No."

I busied myself by reaching for a loofah.

He didn't say anything and I turned around to look at him. He was looking at me with a resigned look.

"Do you want me to get out?"

"No. This is your home, your shower. You have every right to be here."

He didn't say a word and I pretended he wasn't standing there as I began to lather myself. "I'm making you uncomfortable. I'll get out."

I didn't respond, I just let him leave. And when the shower door closed, I gave a sigh of relief. But then I quickly felt disappointment. My emotions when it came to Magnus were so conflicted. I didn't know what I wanted. And clearly, he wasn't happy with that.

I grabbed a robe that I found hanging up and didn't bother looking for anything to wear. I figured Magnus would let me borrow a t-shirt and shorts.

I found him in the kitchen, making toast.

To my surprise he didn't acknowledge my presence. He didn't even look at me.

"You hogged all the toast?" I asked, attempting to make my tone light. I could tell the mood between us had changed. And I knew that was my fault.

"I didn't think you would be interested in sticking around for breakfast," he said succinctly, standing up to go to the refrigerator. He pulled out some orange juice and drank it straight from the jug. He wiped his mouth off with the back of his hand and sat back down and kept eating.

I stood there awkwardly, not knowing how to act or what to say. I didn't know why, but I felt out of place.

"Why'd you agree to spend the night?" he asked, catching me by surprise with his question.

"What?"

"Why did you agree to spend the night?"

"You asked me to," I said, meeting his eyes and seeing regret there.

For some reason, that hurt me. He regretted what happened between us?

"I don't understand you, Lesli," he said gruffly.

"What's that supposed to mean?" I said more testily than I'd intended. Great. I was already getting on the defensive.

"You know what I mean. We spent all night making love to each other, but yet you treat me like a stranger in the morning. We're friends. At least I thought we were and we've been lovers several times over, but yet I still make you uncomfortable?"

I shrugged and avoided his eyes. "It's not you—"

"Then what is it?"

I didn't know what to say. What was my problem? Why was I always pushing Magnus away?

"Are you going to answer me?"

"I don't know what you want me to say," I said truthfully, finally meeting his eyes again. "I don't know why I keep pushing you away Magnus. I really don't. But does it really matter? We're two different people from two different walks of life."

"What does that have to do with anything?" He narrowed his eyes and crossed his arms.

"Everything," I said shortly.

"Explain." His tone was equally curt.

"What don't you understand? We're from two different worlds. I grew up poor in a state no one even thinks of visiting and you grew up rich in a cool, international city. I'm a just a geeky girl who never fit in anywhere and you're Florida's most eligible bachelor. Come on, Magnus. Admit it. We're too different."

"Too different for what?"

"To make this work."

"You haven't even given us a chance."

"There's no need. I already know how it will turn out in the end. I'm not your kind—"

"My *kind*? What the hell are you talking about, Lesli? Is the chip on your shoulder really that big?"

I instantly tensed up. "Yes, yes, it is. If you grew up how I did—"

"And how exactly did you grow up? Because it sounds to me like you had a great childhood. That you grew up with people who loved you and encouraged you to be whoever you wanted to be. So spare me the sob story. You're just making excuses. The only one who feels like you don't belong is you."

His words hit deep. He read me too well and that was scary. I was used to being the outcast. I was used to being the one that didn't fit in. Was I creating that reality here in Florida? Had I been the one to create that reality in school? Had I really been the problem this whole time? Me?

I couldn't refute his words, but that didn't mean that I couldn't be angry.

"You don't know me. You don't know anything about me. So please stop trying to psychoanalyze me."

"Trust me. I wouldn't even try. I don't have a millennium to figure out why you refuse to be happy."

"Are you done?" I said, securing the belt of the robe around my waist with shaky hands.

"No, I'm not."

"Well, I'm done listening." I marched back into his bedroom and resigned myself to wearing the seventies costume I had come in the night before.

To my surprise, Magnus followed.

"So that's it then? You're just going to leave."

"Apparently, you just want to fight. I'm not in the mood for fighting, so yes, I'm going to leave."

He shook his head. "I care about you, Lesli. More than you realize, but for the life of me I can't figure you out."

I ignored him as I began to get dressed. The room was tense with emotion and I could feel it in the air. It made me decidedly uncomfortable.

"I'm just asking for a chance. I feel like I'm always begging you or chasing you."

"Then stop begging me. Stop chasing me," I said viciously. I was getting frustrated, not with Magnus but with myself.

"I can't. It's not that easy for me."

"It's not that easy for you to stop chasing someone who doesn't want anything to do with you?" My comment was a low blow. I knew it was nasty, but I felt like an injured animal and I was just lashing out, rather than face being hurt.

He called me on it. "Stop lashing out and just talk to me. Tell me what's going on in your head."

"I don't want to talk. I'm just not interested in this—" I gestured toward him.

"Not interested in what?"

"A relationship. You. All of it. Ok? That's it. Can we just leave it alone now?"

"No."

"Why not?" I said, turning on him angrily.

He said softly, "Because, against my better judgment, I've fallen for you, Lesli."

I felt like my whole world had shifted out of focus.

My eyes became blurred by tears and a million emotions welled up inside me.

"I got to go," was all I was able to say.

"Aren't you going to acknowledge what I just said?"

I laughed harshly and said, "You've fallen for me, but you've been dating my friend. Ok. Likely story."

"You know my relationship with Violet was just friendly. I was just a placeholder while she waited for her boyfriend to see her with a rich dude on the news."

"My heart goes out to you," I said again in a nasty tone. I got my bag and stomped out toward the door.

"Lesli, come on... just talk to me. Stop running from me. Tell me what you're thinking. Tell me what you're feeling. I know you care about me."

I had my hand on his doorknob when I felt his hand on my shoulder. I wanted to turn around and tell him that I felt the same way, that I wanted something to happen between us too, but I was scared. I was too scared of being happy. I was scared that if I let him into my heart, he would find a reason to leave me. And I didn't know if I could handle that.

"Lesli, don't leave. I love you."

And with those words, my next action was sealed. I couldn't accept Magnus's love. I was too afraid. I was too afraid that one day he would stop loving me and take those very words back.

And so without a word of acknowledgment, I turned

the knob and left. I shut the door behind me and slowly made my way to the elevator. I prayed that he wouldn't follow me and he didn't.

As I stepped into the elevator, I placed my head against the wall and let the tears fall. And as the elevator doors shut, so did the future I had that would contain love.

12

―――――

$\mathcal{I}$ didn't know where to go. I didn't want to face Lacey and Jude or the questions I knew she would have for me. Instead, I called Oliver and he welcomed me.

I sat in his garden just thinking about my life and everything I'd been through recently with the "Magnus Situation" when Oliver decided to join me.

"You're one contemplative lady today."

I sighed. "Yeah."

"Care to share?"

"You wouldn't understand."

"Try me. No, come on. I might be old and weathered, but I know a thing or two about affairs of the heart."

I looked at Oliver's face. He had more wrinkles now than I remembered, but he seemed so happy. I knew it was because of Kat now in his life. They had instantly hit it off and I knew they were talking about marriage, but Kat valued her freedom and wasn't interested. I heard that Oliver respected her decision, so maybe he'd understand my dilemma, even though I was the one running, while he was the one who wanted the relationship.

"I just don't know what I want out of life anymore. All I've been good at is school. It's all I've ever done well. I moved to Florida to try something different. I came to Florida and I got what I wanted. A different life. Adventure."

"And you're upset about that?"

"Yes," I sighed in frustration. "No. I just—life is more complicated now. I've been defined by being the smart girl. The geek. The nerd. But here, I'm just me... but I don't know how to be just me."

"It really sucks when people accept you for who you are and don't put a label on you, doesn't it?" he joked.

I gave a harsh chuckle. "I'm having an identity crisis and I'm only twenty-three."

He shrugged and crossed his ankles. "Better than having one at fifty. Trust me. I know from experience."

"Oh, Oliver, what am I going to do with my life?"

"How about you just stop overanalyzing everything?"

"What?"

"You're a smart young lady. You and Lacey are a lot alike, you know?"

I shook my head. "She's a sassy, determined, take no prisoners, type of girl. I'm more of a fall in line and do whatever comes next type of girl."

"You don't give yourself enough credit. Sometimes you just need to let go and let life happen."

I looked at him again. He was wearing a plain t-shirt with a rainbow-colored Toucan on the front. He had on neon yellow shorts that were threadbare and a pair of gold running shoes. He was also wearing red-tinted sunglasses that resembled the ones Jerry Garcia always wore.

"I wish I could be more like you, Oliver. More carefree, less uptight."

"You're not uptight."

"That's what everyone at school thought."

"You're not in school anymore."

He was so right. I wasn't Lesli, the little girl who didn't belong.

I was just plain Lesli. And hadn't that been enough? I'd made friends: Violet and Maya. Just being Lesli was enough for them. Everyone at work liked me. No one else cared about my IQ or anything. They just liked me for me. Magnus liked me. He accepted me for who I was and instead of embracing that, I'd fought it. Even when I realized how I felt about him, I'd fought those emotions.

My rejection of Magnus had nothing to do with him or his stature in life. It had everything to do with my insecurities. I couldn't love someone else if I didn't even know how to accept myself. And that was the problem. Magnus wasn't the problem. He loved me.

But I didn't believe him, because I didn't really love me. If I couldn't accept myself, then how did I think someone else would accept and love me for me?

"Do you think I should talk to him?"

"Him?" Oliver pretended to not know what I was talking about. Typical Oliver.

"You know... Magnus."

"Why not? That's all up to you."

I nodded. "Thanks for listening, Oliver. I appreciate it. You really helped me figure out some really confusing things."

He patted my hand. "Life is confusing. I get it. Half the time I don't know if I'm coming or going."

I had to laugh. "You're great, Oliver. You really are. Thanks for everything."

"Anytime, my dear." He stood up then and said, "Care to join me for lunch? Kat is making a salad. She promises that it'll be the most delicious salad known to man. It's probably just going to be lettuce and tomatoes, but I'm determined to pretend it's delicious and exotic."

My first inclination was to say no, but I thought better of it. "Why not? Lead the way."

The next day, I drove to the studio where the final episode of Brain Pain's charity event was supposed to be filmed. Oliver had insisted I use one of the cars in his garage. There had been at least five of them, and so I had selected the smallest and least expensive. A Mercedes SUV. I felt so pretentious as I handed the keys to the valet.

Inside, the set was just as busy as before. The host looked calm and relaxed sitting in a lounge chair watching the chaos unfold.

The production assistant Celeste saw me and came right toward me. "It's about time you got here. Where's your partner?"

"I don't know. He's normally early. I'm not sure where he is."

"Aren't you guys a couple?"

"What? No."

"Oh. You two act like a couple, I figured that you were together. Well, you know what they say about assumptions...." She let her voice trail off as she led me to my spot.

Dr. Joseph was there with her partner. They were exactly where they needed to be. Only Magnus was missing. I started getting nervous. Maybe he wouldn't show up. Maybe he hated me so much for how I'd treated him that he was just going to throw the championship.

All those thoughts and more passed through my head before I squashed them. No, Magnus wouldn't do that. No matter how much I messed up, he wasn't self-ish. He wouldn't jeopardize Ophelia's Angels' chance at a million dollars. Magnus was too good a guy to do that.

The production team was giving me a hard time and now people were making phone calls when suddenly Magnus showed up with his personal assistant trailing behind. "He's here. Let's get started," said the personal assistant breathlessly.

"Where were you?" I immediately asked.

He ignored me. "Why does it matter to you?"

"You're my partner," I said. "You matter to me."

He didn't answer me. He just ignored me. I figured I deserved that.

And then, we were on. "Welcome back to Brain Pain. And if you're just joining us. We have with us our four finalists from last week's episode, Magnus and Lesli from Ophelia's Angels and Alexandra and Pete from Cycle Psychos. Alexandra and Pete, what would winning today mean to you?"

Pete talked about the bicycles that the organization refurbished and distributed to poverty-stricken women, men, and children around the world at low to no cost. It was then our turn and we answered the same question.

I answered for our team, saying, "Ophelia's Angels' mission is to provide the elderly with necessities such as food, water, and medication. We would like to expand to every country in the world. By winning today, we can make that happen."

The audience clapped politely and then it was time for the game. We all went to stand at our places in front of the huge glowing buttons that said Brain or Pain.

"It's that time to choose and since Alexandra and Lesli chose last time. We're going to let Pete and Magnus choose this time. So, fellas, what will it be? Will it be pain or brain?"

Magnus without a thought stepped forward. Pete followed, and they were in agreement. They chose Brain.

Apparently, they were nicer than us women.

"And it's time for the brain challenges. Ladies, you're up!"

Magnus and Pete watched from the audience while Dr. Alexandra Joseph and I answered question after question. We were tied by the end of the round. I was just excited that I'd been able to keep up with her.

I said as much to her when we stopped for a commercial break.

She laughed. "Why are you surprised? You were light years ahead of me when you were just a teenager. It was me who was trying to keep up with you during that brain round."

"You remember me?" I couldn't believe it.

She smiled. "Of course, I remember you. You were

one of the smartest young ladies I've ever had the pleasure to teach. And I'm happy to see you developed so much grit and confidence over the years. You've grown up to be quite a force to reckon with, but then again, I always knew you would be."

Before I could say another word, the commercial break was over and our partners were taking our places.

"Good luck," I said to Magnus, and he just grunted. Yeah, he hated me. My hurt heart at the idea, but could I really blame him?

I turned around to look at the audience, some of them had large handwritten signs in their hands that supported various charities, or the signs were hello to the host. Many read, "Good luck, Ophelia's Angels!" and one even read, "Magnus Deacon, you're hot!" I laughed, wondering if Magnus had seen that sign yet and suddenly I had a very, very good idea. Dr. Joseph had said I had been a force to reckon with. And I was going to prove her right.

I signaled for the production assistant Celeste and asked her for exactly what I needed. She looked at me as if I were crazy, but I put my hands together and begged her. "Pretty please, Celeste."

She grudgingly went away and came back with a black marker and a huge piece of paper that was about half the size of my body. I gave her a big smile and got to work.

As big as I could, I wrote exactly how I felt. Then, I positioned myself near the middle of the audience, right in Magnus's line of vision.

He was in the middle of answering a question when he caught sight of my sign. He frowned, missed the question and Pete answered it instead.

It lost us the lead and I started to regret my sign, but I saw the unmistakable smile on Magnus's face as his eyes met mine.

He took his eyes off mine and focused on the next question and to my surprise, he got question after question right. And finally they were tied, but the end of the game was nearing.

"With only ten seconds left in the game, now it's time for the bonus round," said the host. "Winner takes all."

Silence descended over the audience. "Magnus, Pete, the first person to answer this question correctly wins the game. Are you ready?"

The hush over the crowd was deafening and the tension that filled the building was unreal. No wonder Brain Pain was so popular. The drama was more than I could bear.

And finally, the last question was read: "What is the capital of Uzbekistan? Is it Buenos Aires, Tashkent, or Bukhara?"

I knew this one and it took so much self-control not to scream it out.

Both guys hit their buttons at the same time it seemed, but according to the host, Magnus had been faster.

"Is it Bukhara?" he said with a smile, totally confident.

I slowly let my breath out as I sunk into my chair.

"Sorry, Magnus, you're wrong. Pete, you have the opportunity now to win the million dollars for your charity if you can tell us the correct answer."

Pete smiled, looking just as confident as Magnus did a minute ago.

"Is it Tashkent?"

The host took a deep breath and then yelled, "Congratulations to our winners, the Cycle Psychos!"

I clapped politely, but felt terrible for Magnus and more so for Ophelia's Angels. I was sorry it had come to this. We had failed.

I saw Magnus hug Dr. Joseph and shake Pete's hand. The host said goodbye to the audience and then Magnus made his way to me.

I was suddenly nervous, and I wanted to hide behind my sign. Speaking of which, he stopped in front of me and reached for my sign.

"Nice sign. It was very inspirational."

"Not inspirational enough. It distracted you, otherwise, you would have easily won."

He shrugged. "It's not every day that a woman tells you that she loves you in front of a live studio audience."

I looked down at my sign, written from the heart. It simply read, "I love you, Magnus." He pulled the sign out of my hand and pulled me toward him.

Nervously I licked my lips and said, "I'm sorry you lost."

He pulled me closer to him, wrapping me in his arms. "I didn't lose today. As far as I'm concerned, because I have you in my arms, I won." And with that, with the production assistants and stragglers from the audience still remaining, he leaned down and kissed me and what followed was deafening applause.

EPILOGUE

"Have you seen Elvis? Has anyone seen Elvis?" Lacey asked us as she walked back and forth. I knew she was a second from going into panic mode, so I quickly stood up to help her with her search.

Elvis was their new puppy. They had named him Elvis because Las Vegas was where Elvis Presley impersonators frequently performed, and Las Vegas held a special place in Jude's and Lacey's heart. Even though Elvis was a whopping ninety pounds, he could still hide himself very well. I found him a second later with baby Sebastian, who wasn't quite a baby anymore, hiding next to the bed. They were both eating cookies. Peanut butter cookies....

"They're here... both of the little troublemakers," I added. Sebastian giggled and then jumped up to hug me around my legs. He was almost four years old. I couldn't believe how fast time had gone by.

"Auntie Lesli, Elvis is bad."

"Oh, is he?" I laughed.

Sebastian nodded seriously. "He's real, real bad. He ate my cookies."

I frowned, ready to playfully scold Elvis, but then laughed as Elvis rolled over for a belly rub.

"Uh oh, someone wants belly rubs," I said bending down and Sebastian joined me, both of us giggling as Elvis's tongue lolled around and he leaned his head back in blissful abandon.

"You two," Lacey said, shaking her head. "How am I going to get any work done with you two stealing cookies?"

"Not me, Mommy," said Sebastian. "It was Elvis."

Lacey winked at me and then turned back to Sebastian. "So Elvis went into the pantry and took those cookies?"

Sebastian nodded so hard that the bangs on his forehead bounced up and down. He was so cute and looked just like his mom.

"Hmm... I guess I'll have to give Elvis a timeout, right?"

"Yep," Sebastian said with a giggle.

I decided that Lacey could take it from there and I

made my way back to the sofa and seated myself between Oliver and Kat.

They were arguing over wedding invites. Oliver had finally worn Kat down and got her to say yes. The only stipulation is that they would get to maintain separate residences. After all, Kat didn't want to lose her sense of independence. I hoped that I was like Kat when I reached her age.

Sitting across from us was Magnus and Jude. Strangely enough, Jude had been really into helping plan his dad's wedding. I think he wanted to see his father happy.

Speaking of happiness, I couldn't help but stare at Magnus as he slowly organized the wedding invitations by color. He was great. I was discovering new things about him almost every day, it seemed. And I was finding out new things about myself as well. It was safe to say we were growing together.

"Are you ready to head out?" I asked him. We'd been there since early morning. I reached for my bag and remembered that I had something special to give to Sebastian. "Give me a sec," I said to Magnus.

I found Sebastian sitting on his bed trying to read a book. "I have something for you," I said reaching into my bag. I pulled out Mr. Boo and handed him to Sebastian.

"For me?" he asked, hugging it tightly.

I nodded and smiled. Lacey peeked in and said, "Mr. Boo? You're giving up Mr. Boo?" She knew how much the toy had meant to me as a child.

I nodded. "Mom sent him to me in a big box of all my childhood things. But I think this is a better home for him. What do you think, Sebastian?"

"I love Mr. Boo," he said sweetly.

"Yeah, I had a feeling that you would…" I felt myself tearing up and didn't want to embarrass myself by crying in front of a preschooler. I didn't know why I was so emotional. I guess it was because giving my childhood toy away was less about the action and more about what it represented. It represented how I was finally able to move on, to grow up, to become the person I'd dreamed of being.

I gave Sebastian a parting hug, said a final goodbye to Mr. Boo and headed back into the living room where Magnus stood, looking handsome, waiting for me.

"You ready?"

I nodded.

He said goodbye to everyone and as we left said, "Call us if you guys need any more help." He reached for his jacket and together we headed out.

It was a chilly day, especially for South Florida. It was in the low sixties. I liked it and was enjoying the change of weather. Other South Floridians probably disagreed with me as they walked around wearing scarves and down jackets as if it were ten below. I thought it was funny.

I had moved in with Magnus almost six months ago and I didn't regret the decision at all. Waking up next to him every morning was my favorite part of the day.

Not that the rest of my day wasn't also great. I'd taken Maya's job once she was promoted to a new director position that was made possible by an anonymous donation of a million dollars to Ophelia's Angels after we'd lost Brain Pain. It was hard to tell who'd gifted the amount. I figured it was Magnus, but Oliver was equally generous. Neither one would admit to it, so I guess it would always stay a mystery. I could have been way off base though, as it could have just as easily been Misha's husband, Erik. I forgot that my life was now full of billionaires.

I never thought about their net worth, because at the end of the day, they were my friends and my family, not a number. And they were the most down to earth people I knew.

I got into the updated version of Magnus's car and he surprised me by driving to the park where we'd had our first non-date.

"What are we doing here?" I asked surprised.

"We're going to feed the ducks. I think they miss us."

"Miss us? They tried to kill me."

"They were just a little overenthusiastic. Come on."

I followed him, but not happily. The ducks could feed themselves for all I cared. We turned the corner and I noticed that rose petals lined the way toward the pond.

"What happened here?" I wondered out loud. "Did someone have a wedding near the pond?"

And just as I said that I noticed that the gazebo where the teenagers had filmed my disgrace was covered in what seemed to be a million flowers, exotic tropical flowers, romantic roses, and delicate lilies.

He took my hand and pulled me toward the entrance of the gazebo.

"Umm... what's going on?"

I was in awe of how the gazebo had been turned into a little bit of paradise. And then it dawned on me as Magnus lowered himself onto one knee what exactly was happening.

"Oh my God...."

He reached into his pocket and pulled out a ring. "It was my great grandmother's," he said. He laughed wryly. "It was the one thing my mother didn't just give away."

"I'm glad she didn't," I couldn't help but say as I reached for the ring, "Yes, of course, I'll marry you."

He laughed. "I didn't get a chance to ask you yet."

"Oh my gosh. I'm so sorry. Ask me now. Ask me now." I was practically bouncing with excitement.

He couldn't help but laugh again. "Lesli Cabot, will you do me the honor of becoming my wife?"

"Yes! Yes! Yes!" Now I was jumping up and down. He stood up and gathered me in his arms.

"I love you," he said softly against my ear.

"And I love you," I whispered back.

I'd left West Virginia to seek an adventure and I realized that with Magnus, every day of my life with him would be not only an adventure, but an adventure full of love.

DELETED SCENE

He sat in the chair across from the bed watching me as I undressed. I figured he would want to undress me himself, but I was wrong. He just wanted to watch.

My hands shook a little, not in fear, but in excitement as I slid my shirt off first. Then I let my shorts follow, stepping out of them with one smooth motion.

I slid my panties down next, feeling the wetness of my crotch evident on the silk of my panties. I took off my bra then. It joined my panties on the floor and I walked to him, naked and confident, and extended my hand toward him.

He took it and I led him toward the bed. He took a moment to rub his hands across my behind and buried his head in the crook of my neck as he reached around my body and started to fondle my breasts. He squeezed my nipples and I gasped as he released them to cup my breasts.

His touch was warm, smooth, intoxicating. I felt myself growing wet, so wet that I could feel the wetness on my thighs. And then one of his hands found its way to my sex and he started stroking me there. He took his time while nibbling my ear, all the while playing with my clit.

I was breathing heavily and writhing my ass against his throbbing sex when he abruptly stopped and gave me a little shove toward the bed.

I looked at him in confusion and he wordlessly laid down next to me, unzipping his pants. He took his thick cock in his hand and started to stroke it, up and down as he looked at me. His eyes devouring my breasts, my belly, my femininity.

I reached for him then and he took my hand and brought it to his mouth. He lowered himself to his elbow and began to plant little kisses up my arm, the inside of my elbow, before abandoning my arm to kiss my lips.

His kiss was warm, and it held promise. Promise of what? I didn't know, but for a moment time felt suspended as our lips pressed together.

He slowly pulled away and I protested. He laughed gruffly and said, "I want to see you play with yourself."

His request sounded so dirty. So wanton. I was instantly turned on.

I did as he said. I laid down and parted my legs and watched him stroke his dick as he watched me touch my clit.

He licked his lips and I fantasized that those lips were brushing against my femininity. That his fingers were separating the folds of my sex. So I parted my legs wide and began to penetrate myself with one finger as I played with my nipple with the other hand. I became impatient, wanting his hands on me. Wanting his lips on me.

"Kiss me," I said, as he watched me finger myself. He kissed me, starting at my neck and moving forward toward my ears.

I gasped as his lips finally met mine and he stopped stroking himself to grab my breast. I began to draw circles around my clit as he kissed and fondled me. And without warning, I began to come as my sex quivered and my hips shot up on their own accord.

He kept kissing me as he climbed on top of me and slid into me without preamble. He rode me hard, pumping in and out of me, as he continued to hold my face and plant kisses all over my cheeks, my forehead, my chin.

And then when I thought he was about to come, he surprised me by pulling out of me. He slid down my body and began to kiss and suck my sex. He rubbed his face against my pubic area, inhaling the scent of me.

"God, you smell good..." he said softly as he licked my folds, tasting me as if I were some sort of delicacy. As he began to suck my clit, I fondled my own breasts. I squeezed my nipples hard and my thighs shook as he pressed them further apart. The feel of his tongue sliding between the folds of my pussy and circling around my clit was too much to bear. I came quickly, gasping his name. I let go of my breasts and grabbed his head, keeping him still as I bucked against his mouth. I came against his face and he lapped at my wetness greedily.

And then finally, when he was done, he turned me over. Exhausted, I stretched my arms across the bed and kept my face pressed against the mattress, trying to catch my breath.

I was surprised at how long he had been hard already as he pushed into me again. I was so wet that he slid in easily. Between the wetness of his mouth and the wetness of my sex, my entryway was primed for the taking.

He surprised me by stretching forward and pinning my hands with one of his above my head as he fucked me hard from behind. Each one of his thrusts pushed me forward and I began to scream from pleasure as each of his thrusts stretched me, filled me to the point I thought I couldn't accommodate anymore of him. I knew he was long. I knew his cock was thick, but in this position, it felt even bigger, even wider.

At that point, it was like my sex was made for his. And I happily let him have his way with it, moaning as he buried himself inside me, pulled out and thrust back in slowly, stretching me.

And finally, when I thought I couldn't take anymore, he began to speed up and I knew this was no longer about me. It was about him, his pleasure. He was ready to come.

It was tricky, but I reached between us and grabbed his balls. I rubbed them, applied just enough pressure to hear him moan in pleasure.

"Oh God, Lesli..."

He groaned and began to pump into me faster, almost hurting me... getting to that point where pleasure and pain were quickly becoming one. As I started to come again, I screamed his name so many times my throat became hoarse. With one more strong thrust, he came inside of me.

I rotated my hips and moaned as his seed filled me... it was warm and for some reason, the idea of his essence inside me turned me on even more and I came again, the orgasm of all orgasms radiating from my center and spreading through my veins. My entire body began to shake and my head began to explode.

He rolled off me and gathered me into his arms as I waited for the waves of pleasure from the force of my orgasm to subside. I let him cuddle me against his chest and strangely, I felt closer to him at that moment than I ever had before.

I was drowsily stroking his chest and his head was pressed into my neck. We lay like that with me wrapped in his arms.

I felt comforted, protected, cherished.

And I didn't want that feeling to end. As I drifted off, he placed a chaste kiss on my forehead.

"Get some sleep, love."

I fell asleep against his chest feeling many emotions, but in the mist of them all, one emotion stood out. Love.

DARK DESIRES
~ A billionaire dark romance series ~
Dark Desire
Dark Rules
Dark Secret
Dark Time
Dark Truth

BARRE TO BAR
~ A billionaire second chance series ~
Dancing With Lies
Dancing With Temptation
Dancing With Doubt
Dancing With Guilt
Dancing With Redemption

TWISTED INTENTION
~ A billionaire revenge romance series ~
Twisted Beauty
Twisted Love
Twisted Fate

Mafia's Obsession
~ A hot mafia romance series ~
Mafia's Dirty Secret
Mafia's Fake Bride
Mafia's Final Play

Screaming Demons
~ An MC romance series full of suspense ~
Rough Start
Rough Ride
Rough Choice
Rough Patch
Rough Return
Rough Road
Rough Trip
Rough Night
Rough Love

Standalone Contemporary Romance
Billionaire in Vegas
Billionaire Hunt

Billionaire's Game
Billionaire Retreat
Billionaire On Air
A Chance To Love
Somebody To Love
Not Mine To Love

Check out Summer's entire collection at
www.summercooper.com/books

www.ingramcontent.com/pod-product-compliance
Lightning Source LLC
Chambersburg PA
CBHW051304210726
48287CB00002B/661